ASTRIDE

AN EROTIC JOURNEY OF DAYDREAMS AND DELICIOUS DELIGHTS

Christine Leov Lealand

PENGUIN BOOKS

PENGUIN BOOKS

Penguin Books (NZ) Ltd, cnr Airborne and Rosedale Roads, Albany,
Auckland 1310, New Zealand
Penguin Books Ltd, 80 Strand, London, WC2R 0RL, England
Penguin Putnam Inc, 375 Hudson Street, New York, NY 10014, United States
Penguin Books Australia Ltd, 250 Camberwell Road, Camberwell,
Victoria 3124, Australia
Penguin Books Canada Ltd, 10 Alcorn Avenue, Toronto,
Ontario, Canada M4V 3B2
Penguin Books (South Africa) Pty Ltd, 5 Watkins Street,
Denver Ext 4, 2094, South Africa
Penguin Books India (P) Ltd, 11, Community Centre, Panchsheel Park,
New Delhi 110 017, India

Penguin Books Ltd, Registered Offices: Harmondsworth, Middlesex, England

First published by Penguin Books (NZ) Ltd, 2001

3 5 7 9 10 8 6 4

Illustrations by Judy Lambert
Author photograph by Brett Whincup
Designed by Mary Egan
Typeset by Egan-Reid Ltd

Printed in Australia by McPherson's Printing Group

All references to and quotes from 'The Rocky Horror Picture Show' are
from the original musical play and lyrics by Richard O'Brien; screenplay by
Jim Sharman and Richard O'Brien.

ISBN 0-14-100528-9
www.penguin.co.nz

to
JRM
beloved inspiration

Don't dream it — be it.
— *The Rocky Horror Picture Show*

To love is to receive a glimpse of heaven.
— *Karen Sunde, playwright*

Contents

I am decomposing
Soft
Ready
Fermenting

Peel my mushroom
Mouth my ripe
Slice into soft, slick
With your sharp

I am hot and willing
Open
Firm
Moist

Oyster lips dripping
Snowmelt pours
Firm as warm ripe peach
Mushed melon

Incise your mark
Pink wax soft

I'm astride
Groove me

Chapter 1

SOLO MUM

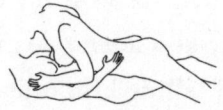

'Best thing I ever did – leave my husband!' Anne looked at the long sheaf of documents in her hand. At last the final separation papers had been forwarded by her lawyer. The bill had arrived months ago. Bloody lawyers! Always cost you money you didn't have. The good thing was that these papers confirmed 6-year-old Sara and 2-year-old Jamie officially in her custody. The fact that they were to spend alternate weekends and school holidays with their dad was finally written down in black and white.

For the first time in the past year she began to feel a sense of security. Satisfaction filled her as she poured hot water into her cup, dissolving the instant coffee. Stirred in a spoon of sugar and poured in milk. The benefit didn't give her enough spare money to buy real coffee so instant it had to be.

She sipped the hot drink as she shuffled through the

papers again. Ahhh, so good, the bitter bite of the coffee and the separation agreement signed at last. Now she could get on with her life, knowing that she would be a free woman in a year or so. Well — as free as anyone could be with two young kids to care for and love.

She sighed as she picked up the loaded washing basket and followed Jamie as he crawled outside into the bright Nelson sunlight. The joke's on my ex, she mused. Joe hassled me endlessly about who was in my head, after I made the mistake of telling him one of my fantasies. He demanded to know who and what turned me on and why. Accused me constantly of being a slut. She laughed. But I haven't had a man since I walked out on Joe a year ago. It's a good feeling too. I've been happy to be alone, especially after what he did to me, and besides, who would I want? What kind of man would suit me?

She began to peg the wet clothes out on the line as Jamie toddled over the grass pursuing the cat. A young man, perhaps someone my own age? What about a different race? A Polynesian guy, some of them are really sexy. Is sexy what I really want? Maybe I need someone older than me, 30 maybe, or 35 — even 40 years old. Someone who doesn't drink or smoke. Who would woo me over a few months with phone calls, attentiveness, caring and friendship. A man who, when he touched me — I'd feel safe, cared for, loved. Calm in his arms.

Not nervous and uptight, wondering what he's going

to do next. Not wondering if, when he drank too much, as Joe always did — if he'd pick a fight with another guy. Or if when I managed to get him home safe, he'd pick a fight with me, shouting and shoving me around. Wouldn't matter what I did, he'd always end up grabbing me by the hair and ramming my face into a door. His favourite form of torture.

Silly, ignorant me. I took it because I was pregnant and so tired I couldn't fight back. Didn't dare fight back. I'd married this beast, hadn't I? I believed I had to sleep in the miserable bed I'd accidentally made for myself. Old-fashioned, cruel rules to live by.

Hah! I wish I'd known then what I know now. That if I'd gone to get help, counselling, to the Women's Refuge, I could have helped both of us. It's too late for us now, but at least Joe's going to anger management. Well that's what his mum tells me. What good it will do I don't know. I hope it means Jamie won't see him abusing any other women.

When I think back to what he did to me I get so angry sometimes I feel I'd like to kill him. What a fool I was getting pregnant even once to an abusive bastard like Joe. Huh! Then I let myself have Jamie to try to keep the relationship together!

She picked up another handful of pegs and began hanging up the wet nappies, pegging them neatly corner-to-corner.

I've grown up a lot in the last year, I hope. Kids don't prevent bad things from happening in a marriage, I've found that one out the hard way. I was really gutless until I finally found the strength to leave Joe. I only managed it with the support of a counsellor, my family and friends. I want to get myself up on my feet now. Train for something, do a computer course, cook more, find a man who will love me, if one of them exists.

I know Kate, Michelle and Mum will be thrilled I want to get out of the old solo mum slog. My family have always been so caring, deeply loving to me. I'm very lucky there.

My best friends, Tina and Lynne, will help me too. Even though they know I'll never be a feminist like they are, in their different ways. Tina's never been married, I don't know how she avoided that, probably by having a different guy every month for the last ten years. And Lynne, well when she came out as a lesbian — who was surprised? No one. Not even her dad.

At least now I'm free to have some fun!

She giggled, peering up at the sunny sky, revelling in the freedom which now seemed to open up the universe to her. Blue, so blue the sweet high summer sky. It seemed full of promise and she felt warm and sunny throughout her body. The sun shone like a bright blade so she squinted her brown eyes as she pegged the wet clothes out steadily. A sharp dry wind blew in from Tasman Bay, snapping the towels and nappies, flicking Anne's long golden-brown hair around her face and shoulders. Jamie looked up at her and laughed as he tipped the pink pegs out all over the rough grass. He gurgled with joy as the cat pounced on the pegs and flicked several under the dahlia bush which was in bud, ready to push out dozens of bright orange blooms.

Anne sat down and watched them play. 'Throw the peg to the cat like this, Jamie,' she coaxed, showing him, and he threw a pink peg at the cat. The cat leapt high, curving her body around like an eel, batting each one down out of the air like she was catching fluorescent birds. Each peg had to have a dispatching bite or two before she was ready to attack the next. Soon the grass was covered with pegs.

The cat tired of the game and disappeared. Jamie crawled under the dahlia, crushing part of it with his heavy body, trying to follow the cat under the fence. Anne picked up the pegs and finished hanging up the nappies.

Mum asks me why I don't use disposables but I take pleasure in pinning Jamie into clean double naps each night, knowing I am not polluting the planet with plastic. It's one of the few pleasures I get these days now I've got no money to come and go on. Feeling good hanging up the washing and growing fresh healthy veggies in the garden. A feeling of self-sufficiency, of having control over something for once. Of doing a little more than *just* managing to cope on a government benefit.

My cooking saves me too. Using my hands, head and

heart, sharp knives, fresh food from my garden. Wooden stirrers made from driftwood rata found on Tahunanui beach when Sara was a baby. Using simple things and good ingredients to make delicious food for my babies, that's most of my joy these days.

Suddenly she thought of sex. Of kisses especially. Of *his* kisses. The man who can kiss me the way I grew up knowing I *could* be kissed.

His warm mouth pressed into mine, melting me with his touch, with the silent speech of his lips. His arms tight around me, wanting me, desiring me, whispering through his kiss about the hot sexy things he wants to do with me. Ahhhh . . . Anne took a deep breath as she pulled Jamie out of the dahlias.

My ex kissed me like that only once. It hooked me to him for years in the hope that more of this soft, enveloping, loving, lip-to-lip communion would be forthcoming any moment. Any moment! Hah! I can remember it now. That was when I fell in love with him. The moment of that singular kiss. Well it must have been a mistake, an accident, Joe kissing me like that. It was the universe tricking me, because it never happened again. Oh for just *one* perfect kiss! No! Not just one, one of anything is never enough! I want more, I want millions of kisses! I want them all, all the time!

She picked Jamie up and moved through the garden to the house. How silly to think that one kiss could satisfy me! I used to think that when I was a kid. I don't think I have *ever* been satisfied. Hell, I've had years of Joe and his lust. His clumsy unbearable version of a fuck. Whatever he did and however he did it never satisfied me. I always wanted more but I quashed those feelings, my true desires. I knew I'd never get my needs met by him and it was useless to ask for anything. I'd almost always get abused for asking. Only sluts want orgasms and cuddles afterwards.

Yet because I married him I always felt that I *should* get everything I needed from him. Well I learned that lesson. Learned it well by erasing all my needs until I thought I didn't have any left. That's how I survived. 'Strange isn't it?' she said to Jamie, 'Strange my little darling how much happier I am now, living alone with you and Sara. I'm so much happier now than I ever was with daddy around.'

Anne got the stroller out and strapped Jamie into it. She had to walk down to the service station to get fresh bread and milk. Sometimes she jogged behind the stroller. Jamie hated it when they shopped because his mother would never allow him out of the trolley to wander the store because inevitably he'd pull things off the shelves. He couldn't help himself. She always made sure he wasn't hungry when they got there but Sara had introduced him to the joys of sweets. He knew all about the sticky muffins, the ice-cream and cakes, the lollies at the end of the counter; he would always want one of everything to take home. He sucked his sweets with totally focused enjoyment. 'Mmmmmmm, mmmm, mmm,' he would hum like a shout of delight, of surprise that something so yummy could exist. Anne wished she could feel that taste again, be like a baby when the first taste of anything really *is* the first taste.

They walked quickly down the country lane towards the main road. I'm like my baby son, I'm dying for the first taste of something I've never had: sex with someone other than Joe, she thought, stretching her legs.

The road painters were parked down the road. Painting the white stripes of the zebra crossing to the tiny post office. Orange cones set out. Yellow lights on the truck flashing. Paint guns hissing as the compressor thudded. Jamie loved trucks.

'Uck! T'uck!' Jamie crowed happily, pointing at it with his chubby fingers. They stopped and watched the two men. They were stripped to the waist in the hot sun. One dark and one fair; both bronzed and muscular. They set out the stencils and began to spray the white paint, their boots splattered with white. Loud rock music roared out from their truck as they worked. The rhythm of the beat rocked Anne.

She stood on the footpath, hesitating, jiggling the stroller. Longing tautly but afraid of the consequences. Longing for those two men, those two artists who daily

18

painted divine smooth white and yellow curves on the road, dots and dashes down the centre. Their work guiding her car home safely, delineating the upward swooping curves of the hills and the downward runs. Preventing accidents with paint. They were powerful men, those road painters.

She looked at them and longed for their hot male minds and bodies to notice her. Put down their spray wands, turn off the thudding compressor and take her. Lift her up against the bonnet of the truck, rip all her clothes off her and kiss her. One caressing her mouth and the other buried in her cunt. Their huge hard cocks erect and throbbing for her. All for her.

She wanted to kneel between them and suck each cock in turn. One would have a long slim penis, the other a short fat one and she'd swoon, her desire making her slick, painting her thighs and cheeks pink with desire. Oh! I want them. You sexy hunks — you road markers, I want you to leave your white stripes on me, in me. Take me! Lean me over a road sign and part my thighs, slowly push that big fat cock into my desperate welcoming body. Ahhh . . . Anne gasped and jiggled the stroller faster. Jamie repeated 'Ook mum! — t'uck,' over and over again as if he knew she wasn't really seeing that incredibly important truck.

She turned away, knowing her desires were misplaced. She wanted those bronzed sweaty bodies, but then she was so frustrated she wanted *any* man. Any man at all — well, almost. Tears of frustration brimmed up in her eyes. The road painters hadn't even glanced up at her and Jamie. Amazing they can't feel my lust, she thought. Even though it's as hot as a blowtorch pointed at them.

When I'm horny like this it's like having PMT only worse. Sex is all I can think about. I get really crabby with the kids for just being kids. It's not their fault I get like this, an old bag who smacks Jamie when he's been silly. Usually I wouldn't dream of hitting my darlings but it's all because I'm dreaming of lovemaking, of being desired, of having a man who would call me 'beloved' or 'darling' and mean it.

I want — I need — I want to know a man to the depths of my being. I want it so badly . . . she walked faster and faster, trying to outrun herself. Wanting to escape her needs.

❧

The phone rang as Anne walked into the cool dark kitchen of the old wooden farm cottage she rented. 'Hello? Hi mum.' She put Jamie into his highchair and gave him a piece of carrot as she made him sandwiches, the phone tucked under her chin. 'Yes mum, no mum.' She worked swiftly as Jamie began to struggle to stand up in the highchair.

'No Jamie,' she said firmly, putting his sandwiches down in front of him.

'Yes, the separation documents came today. It's all OK. I won't argue with it at all. Joe gets access with the kids in the school holidays and on weekends when he's not working, which probably won't be many.' She listened a moment. 'That's not true, mum,' she said firmly. 'Joe's just fine with the kids. Why shouldn't he be? He's their dad and he has a right to see them. Just because he abused me doesn't mean he'll abuse the kids, you know.' She listened again.

'Let's not discuss it any more, mum. You know that if anyone talks to the authorities about abuse, the kids will get put through hours of interviews and analysis and our lives won't be our own any more. *NO!*' firmly, 'I don't hate Joe enough to do that to him. He's their dad and they have a right to see each other, and besides, I need a break from them. I need time to get my own life sorted out. Maybe even find a boyfriend, someone I can really love.'

Jamie threw the mangled remains of his lunch on the floor and attempted to climb out of the highchair once more. She leaned down and set him free.

'OK, I'll come and cook dinner for you next week if you can help me out with petrol. The tank's virtually empty and there's no money till tomorrow but that's pretty well all spent already. Yeah, OK, see you then mum — and mum? — *please* don't invite yet another single guy to dinner with us. It's too embarrassing for me. Thanks.' She sighed as she clicked the handset off.

She looked forward to getting the chance to cook uninterrupted while grandma and her younger sisters Kate and Michelle spoiled Sara and Jamie. How lucky I am to have my family, she thought, smiling. Mum worries too much. I know Joe won't hassle me now, it's all over and done between us, and anyhow there's a protection order on him to keep us safe if he gets too drunk or crazy again. I have to trust him, trust that he won't hurt his kids. I couldn't cope at all if I didn't trust some part of Joe.

Oh – I'm lonely! I want a man who will take me in his arms and hold me close. Give me a feeling of calm. I long to feel warm, safe and loved. She picked Jamie up and danced with him around the kitchen, dodging the mushy sandwiches on the floor.

If I had a man we would dance slowly, sensuously, his hips pressed to mine and he'd gaze into my eyes and say, 'Anne, you are the most sexy, lovely woman in the world.' Then I'd smile a sparkling smile of fabulous happiness because I would know he really meant what he said. Ahhh, and then, *then* he'd kiss me that delicious kiss of desire as we danced and I'd float off into the love universe swinging around and around that exquisite Disney castle. Exploding with fireworks, sprinkling fairy dust with Tinkerbell, flying with Peter Pan to a never-never land of eternal happiness with my lover . . . Jamie squealed with joy and excitement as she whirled him around the kitchen in her arms.

Anne sighed, gave Jamie's wet, smeary face a kiss, put him down and knelt to pick up the mess he'd made off the floor. Then she stood, tossed the mushy bread in the compost bucket and made herself a sandwich.

I wonder if I could ever meet an affectionate, warm, passionate, helpful man like the one in my childhood daydreams? Lynne reckons I should be a lesbian like her. The description of the man I want sounds more like a woman to her than a man. She says there aren't any violent women but I dunno, women don't hesitate to lash out sometimes. When I think of even the slightest possibility of being beaten again I feel pale and scared and all I want to do is run and hide. I've never met a woman I fancied, either. It would seem strange, being hit on by a woman. Lynne is happy with her choices but that is her, this is me.

Nope. I will just dream, dream of that ideal man, a bit taller than me but not much. It'd be great to have a lover whose hips met mine, just so. Whose lips were mobile and sexy, soft and warm. Maybe with a moustache, maybe even a beard. Joe was always clean-shaven, very picky about how he looked. He didn't look it but he was a drunk through and through. Appearances can be very deceptive.

Maybe I'd like a man with one of those close-clipped beards, just kinda silky and soft, blonde or red. I've always had a soft spot for redheads. I met a guy called Red, once. He sat beside me and played his guitar. I really liked the music and Red's company but I'd just met Joe back then. He was watching me, scowling at me and — shit! I'm just realising it! I felt afraid of him then, even before we really began going out together.

I remember he glared at Red sitting beside me at the party so I shifted away. Some part of me didn't want to offend Joe at that point. Maybe I realised he'd pick a fight or hassle me even when I was really gone on him. Hell, it would have been great if he *had* picked on Red or me then. I might have had enough incentive to leave the asshole and find someone better. Maybe.

He only started beating me when I was pregnant with Sara. He couldn't handle people making a fuss of me and not him, so he made up for it by taunting and hassling me. Needling me and putting me down, just for fun. Always winding up punching me or threatening to hit me, and me in tears. I tried everything — agreeing with him, disagreeing, locking myself in the loo. Wouldn't matter what I did, it always earned me a roughing-up and then, the morning after, he'd make a humble apology and then force sex on me to make up — it made me sick. I made myself sick letting him do that to me for nearly eight years.

She shuddered and shook her head as she began to move around the house, putting piles of folded children's clothes away in drawers. All these modern appliances and we still haven't done away with the need to spend a lot of time putting things away where you can find them again.

She checked on Jamie; he was happily drawing with his crayons on the newsprint roll that lay on the kitchen floor. 'Good boy. Would you like to draw me something? You're amazing,' she said as she picked up another pile of clothes.

Tina warned me about Joe, way back then, at the beginning. She was so right. I'm glad she's still my friend. I've learnt that people don't warn you about someone being bad for you just for the fun of it. You may not like them for sticking their necks out but most of the time they have a point. Tina cares about me and wasn't just casually making trouble.

She really meant that Joe was a *problem*, she'd heard about Joe from her brothers. They drank at the same pubs as Joe and recognised the animal they were dealing with. Stupid, in-love young me. Couldn't see that they knew things about Joe I couldn't possibly know.

It must have been hell for her, watching things get worse and worse for me as time went on. She's been my friend through thick and thin and boy, was she happy when I told her I'd kicked Joe out. She brought the champagne round immediately.

Best thing I've ever done, getting rid of Joe. I see that now. I can feel myself starting slowly to flower, to spread tentative wings. I'm beginning to see happiness not as a fantasy but maybe as something *I* can have. For *me*.

The phone rang.

'Hey girl!' Tina's cheerful voice sounded in her ear. 'Guess what?'

'What?'

'I just dumped Dwayne today.'

'Oh — well, how many's that this year?'

'Awwww . . . I dunno. You tell me, you always do.'

'One a month is what I make it, quite regular all year. Poor buggers. That one you had a couple of months ago, what was his name — Thomas?'

'Gosh I don't remember that far back!' laughed Tina. 'What about him?'

'Well *he* really cared about you, but as always, you didn't give a damn about him.'

'Ohhhhh . . .' Tina was silent for a few moments. 'Do you want to know what was wrong with Thomas and Dwayne?'

'No. I don't want to know,' said Anne firmly. 'Please don't tell me. I'll either get frustrated or jealous or maybe both. Thomas was gorgeous and you were crazy to throw him over like that. Of course I couldn't have the poor heartbroken fellow. After you'd finished with him he would never look in my direction. Anyway I don't want to think about your ex-boyfriends today. I have to go and see WINZ tomorrow. Try to get some extra petrol money from them. I have to get Sara to school and there seems to be no way to do it except drive there every day.'

Tina laughed contemptuously. 'Well good luck, Anne.

Don't you have an advocate, someone out to bat for you and what you need? The wankers at WINZ just don't tell you what you are entitled to these days and even when you *do* know, actually *getting* the money out of them is like squeezing a block of concrete for gold.'

Anne sighed, feeling like her hands were tied. 'I haven't got an advocate yet, I hope I won't need one. I know that living here is marginal but I love it so much. The garden is fertile, the house is just the right size; cheap rent, it's quiet and safe for the kids. All I need is about ten more dollars a week so I can get Sara to school, that's not a lot to ask is it?'

'You might as well ask your case worker to give you ten bucks out of his own wallet, that's how they'll act, you know. Not as if you have a right to the benefit, which you do, but as if they had to cough up for it out of their own wages. Silly buggers.'

'Yeah, I know. When I first went there I was made to feel like I'd just robbed a bank or something, when I applied for the benefit. All the questions made me feel like I was a criminal, as if I was ripping off the system just by applying for support to bring up Jamie and Sara.'

'Yep – that's how they are! Gotta go, Anne. The work phone is ringing. Chin up – seeya.' The phone clicked and was dead.

Chapter 2

WINZ

The fresh green beans from the garden filled the bowl to the top. Anne looked happily at them and decided — yes, I want to make more than good old steamed beans again. So she sat down to look through the recipe books for something new, something delicious to make with them and found a recipe for green bean salad. Hmmm . . . steam them, cool, chop onion finely, add to the beans with slices of capsicum and a peppery vinaigrette . . . mmmm.

Her mouth watered and she thought how wonderful it would be to have a loving man to share this meal. How proud she felt to be able to feed her children on the produce from her garden. She had dug and planted the garden all by herself and it had provided greens and fruit all year.

Bugger those bastards at WINZ. She was surviving

without them, but only thanks to her family. She sighed and rubbed her eyes, they were sore and puffy. She had cried after coming out of the WINZ office today. A lot of people cried, or got angry and broke things, beat up their kids or partners after visiting a welfare office.

She had asked for an extra allowance so she could take Sara to school by car. The officer flatly refused her any extra money and curtly told her to take Sara to a closer school. 'There *is* no closer school,' explained Anne desperately, wishing she'd brought along a map to show this cold-voiced immovable person exactly how far Sara had to go to get to school.

'Bus, then,' said the officer.

'There are no buses either,' replied Anne, miserably. 'I've tried getting her a ride with some local kids but they are all high school kids and have different times and holidays.'

'Move into town then,' said the officer, not wanting to help at all. Anne sat stock-still, seeing her lovely little cottage and the garden she had worked so hard on drifting into the past because she had to move into town to a grotty old shack at twice the rent because this cheapskate welfare officer wouldn't give her any help when she desperately needed it.

'If I did that then I'd have to apply for a rent allowance,' she explained patiently. She could see that her case officer would not help her, even though she knew she

29

was entitled to travel assistance. She despaired too, because she knew that unless the officer moved on from this WINZ office, she was stuck with their unsympathetic attitude for the foreseeable future. Or at least until Jamie was at school. Welfare didn't pay for childcare so that she could get a part-time job.

'Nonsense! You won't be getting a rent allowance from *me*! Get yourself sorted out and report back in a month,' said the case officer curtly and left her sitting forlornly in the grey interview room.

She was humiliated by her need for the extra money and the way her case officer had not even bothered to consider her request.

Maybe I could home-school Sara . . . could I do that? Approach the school board and ask if someone can help me? Tears burned in her eyes like soap as she considered the bleak future of making do for years on end until Jamie was at school. Enforced poverty with no money for gifts or clothes. No dinners at her sister's or mother's without them helping out with the petrol; and with the huge registration fees and other running expenses it was looking like she couldn't afford to keep her car going much longer.

The bleakness took all the shine off the fresh green beans and she began sadly to top and tail them, slicing them into the steamer while slowly her mind drifted off . . .

Chapter 3

MAN DREAM

To stand on a broad old stone bridge. The hot sun sparkling on the wide river flowing under her as she stared down into its depths. Behind her she felt the prickle of people passing by. Beautiful old buildings lined the riverbank in either direction and her heart beat loudly as she thought this *must* be Paris. City of wet hot loving. Of available men who look exotic and powerful like James Bond but have glossy black skin, shaved heads or long, luxurious, lusty hair. Men who will do anything for me, wine and dine me, give me flowers, kiss me for hours, adore my naked body . . . ahhh . . . Paris. Is it springtime or just my dream giving me spring fever?

A man stops walking and stands beside me, he leans on the balustrade too, gazing down into the water. He wants to talk to me, I can tell. I smile. I like to talk to men, and although mum always said never talk to strange men

— well, how is a girl ever going to get to know anyone? Perhaps strangers are the best to talk to, safer because there is no risk, not like men I do know. I know too much about them and I don't fancy any of them. Familiarity sure breeds contempt.

I sneak a look at him, and he sneaks a look at me at just the same moment. My brown eyes gaze into his brown eyes and we laugh. Shocked by the coincidence that isn't such a strange thing. It's not unusual for two people to look up at the same moment and glance at each other.

His white teeth look lovelier than if they were on a pale-skinned person. What is he? Arab, Tunisian? Moroccan? How would I know? I come from New Zealand, an exotic place to the denizens of Paris. Boring to me, but mysteriously unknown and alien to them.

His hair is perfumed with some delightful cologne I've never come across before. A smell that seems to be the odour of hot sex, the taint of love to me. Is it cinnamon? Cloves and linseed? Anise and saffron? The smell of sex . . . what exactly is it? My body begins to scent herself with my own sexed odour. Can he smell me? Do I smell as exotic and erotically interesting to him?

He is tall, well he seems taller than I am. I see his body rippling under that white shirt, forearms full of taut lines, blood thrusting through veins; his body full of masculine promises. His blue jeans moving over rippling-thick, strong muscle beneath. My body tenses, visioning the

delights of his body serving mine totally. Allowing myself
to surrender to his strength, his desire, his heat in the
sunshine of a foreign day where time has a different
meaning and the washing machine doesn't need to be fed
and unloaded. Oh! Those long sensual dark fingers
exploring my every cleft, his tongue following on close
behind.

I run my tongue over and over my lips, tracing those
fine ultra-sensitive edges between rosy skin and cheek,
hoping my black beau will do this to me. As he leans down
over me I want him to lovingly trace my eyes, my lips, my
ears and nose, with his firm moist tongue. Enclosing that
tongue are perfectly white teeth, his mouth finished off
with warm soft full lips which whisper in exotic languages.
French, Arabic, German. Whatever it is — it is foreign to
me. Exciting to me, uneducated New Zealander that I am,
hardly acquainted with any language but English and I'm
not great at that: ask my poor old English teacher.

Now we are in a restaurant and my dream lover places
a bowl of golden soup in front of me. *Mourtayrol*, he says it
is called. He made it himself using saffron grown on his
parents' farm somewhere in Europe. He can cook as well
as I can, both of us creative and self-taught. We discuss
cooking as he slides down into his chair, showing off his
strong thighs, the sweet bulge of his groin, and slowly,
looking deep into the other's eyes, we sip and sip at the
soup which slides into the mouth like a savoury heaven for

the tongue. My mouth waters even as I eat it. My stomach mourns for the end of the bowl of soup even as it is satiated by golden delight.

He smiles with all of his face: eyes and mouth, brows and teeth. I dissolve into sexual joy. Anticipating the pleasures his glinting teeth, sparkling promise-filled eyes and strong lusty body suggest to me. I adore his enjoyment and lust; his voice deep, husky, full of longing. Teasing and arousing me all at once. Speaking of desire, its taste and texture, smell and bite. Of how he desires me. Then, most interesting of all, of what we will do when we are alone together.

He tells me about his home in some exotic city where he wants to travel with me, live in a yurt on the plains and make love all day, every day. Cook exquisite meals and feed the locals every night with different dishes which will delight and challenge them. I am to provide exotic South Pacific cuisine to augment his European knowledge. I am beginning to love his voice, his body, his hands and eyes wanting me, loving me. I adore his sharing himself unstintingly with me — he's teaching me to do the same: to share myself with him over and over, deeper and deeper; faster, slower, longer and sweeter.

Sweet as crunchy caramel threads laid on baklava in the heat of summer. My mouth aches, watering, wanting his dream of me, of us. Cooking and sex, lust and hunger, desire and satiation. So close, so close to each other these twin drives of the body, which closely involve the mind.

You are what you eat, but how much more are you what and who you love and make love to?

I look back at my relationship with Joe. How making love to him was never an act of love, more an act of plunder on his part and of helplessly accepting brutalisation on mine. What an awful picture this gives me of myself! No wonder I have been sick so long.

Sick and tired, bored and encircled with walls which I couldn't see were only inches high. At any time, if I had had the strength, I could have leapt beyond the power of his bullying hands. For years I didn't see or understand that I *could* jump and find another place, a place of safety and love that belongs to me. A place I deserve.

Now, to fire me, deeply, truly, I need a man's desire. His true masculine lust. And by that I mean his lust to pleasure me and teach me to pleasure him. When his desire dies then as a woman in relation to him I cease to exist. My body has never been of use to me as an object of pleasure and I don't want invisibility any more. I was made for desire and longing and then, ultimately, fulfilment — whatever that is. I want to experience˘ what fulfilment might feel like. Oh, to have no needs because they are all satisfied!

So — love. So — lust. So — desire. I feel like I am always hungry. Needing love to be alive as if I were a vehicle needing refuelling. Filled with petrol before my car will go. The spark-plugs given a charge, the starter motor kicked over, the battery filled with energy.

So far my car is unused, almost fresh out of the box, test-driven once or twice and then garaged. Or maybe marriage to Joe is better described as my being parked in the chook house. Suffering the results of years of being shat upon and corroded, perched on and used, but not for the purpose I was designed for, oh no. No delicious speeding down the highways of pleasure and delight for me, no journeys of discovery to find my top speed, my best cornering abilities, my limits fording streams, my best position to catch the sun.

No runs on beaches risking rust, no exhilaration doing the ton down the main street of some tiny town. Tyres unworn, lips unkissed, needs unmet. I fell asleep, was battered by a bad dream of eight years and I've just woken up – but to what?

What will I discover now I am out of jail, out of the pen and standing free in the sunlight once more?

Oh – there's always the price to pay, always. In any relationship the price of boredom, satiation, violence, pregnancy, disease maybe. I know I've paid the price without any of the advantages accruing to me. It's so long since I had sex it feels like my vagina has healed over completely. As if I were one of those African women who has had all her intimate parts removed and sewn up into a blank nothing. Nothing but a scar.

So, scarred though I am, I'm agreeing once more to risk again, pay again. Pay in passion, emotion, heart, mind and body just to feel a dark foreign man's horny, exotic loving. The kind of heart-stopping man mum warned me about.

The kind of man who has me melting when I see him standing wild and strong on a street corner catching the bus, waving to me. The kind of man who startled me three days in a row with his beauty and smile, his dreams and desires. We agreed to meet once more, the final time before I made my decision to leave with him forever and — I waited for hours, all day at the appointed place, and he never showed up.

I never found him ever again in that huge city. Paris, treacherous city. Even though I desperately searched for him, eyes ceaselessly seeking, walking the streets full of people from every nation of the world. Taking the Metro, haunting the restaurant where we ate the soup. Seeking endlessly for that one man who evoked the animal, sexual woman in me; brought that deep low call of desire from my throat, a low vibrating coo of satisfaction as his sperm dissolved within me and for a few impossibly perfect moments I was one with the universe and him until in the inevitable ultimate betrayal he becomes limp and his body falls from my body.

37

Anne sighed and put the finished beans on to steam. To be 'lightly killed' as her mother would say. She sat down on the kitchen stool and began to make the dressing. I'm just a bloody dreamer, she thought. My imagination is running wild with my emotions. When I hear the history of 'Bolero' on the national programme; or watch the sexy ads on TV and the soft-porn movies which hint at desires I have never discovered. Showing me the potential of passions that have passed me by.

Damn it! I get *so* frustrated I have to work hard controlling my temper. I have to work hard not to take my tensions out on the kids. They don't deserve to bear the brunt of my frustration. I have emotions and passions that need another adult body and mind present in my life to be truly met.

The touch of a body who wants to touch me, the contact of a willing, loving being is what I starve for and no amount of food or solitary sex can provide that for me. Television and masturbation are a boring combo.

Strange, when I think of it, I was often tense like this when I was with Joe. Needing more, instinctively knowing there *is* more, but trying to control myself. Telling myself that just because I was married that it was — *must* be — all perfect. Had to be good, didn't it? Good man, great kids, what more could I want? Selfish bitch wanting more, daring to need what I didn't have.

The steamer hissed gently and tears fell down Anne's

cheeks. What am I gonna do? What *can* I do with two kids to care for? I hope Joe can have them this weekend. Maybe Tina, Lynne and I can go out — I need to relax and have fun.

Chapter 4

THE PERKS OF
A CORDON BLEU CHEF

Anne woke with a gasp — another sharp cry came from the room next door. Jamie was awake, or at least crying out. She sighed and stretched, pulling herself out of her deep before-dawn sleep and fell immediately into her solo-mum loop of frustrated wishing. How great it would be to have someone to lie beside her. Who could take turns going to get Jamie up with loving words. Strip off his wet nappies, kiss and coo to him and bring his hot, damp, squirming little body back into bed with them to snuggle up for more much-needed sleep.

Instead, morning after morning, she couldn't ignore her responsibility. Not for so much as one day of the year unless the kids were visiting their dad or staying over with her mum. No holidays, no time off from parenting for the solo mum or dad. Holidays had been few and far between in the past year.

She sat up grumpily. Too little sleep. It *always* felt like too little sleep, even when she was sure she'd managed eight or nine hours. It was Jamie waking in the night or Sara's nightmares which kept her from sleeping.

That critical inner voice said, 'It's your own fault. You should have stayed with their father.' Anne cried back at herself, 'What???!! Stay with someone who was abusing me, someone who never, not even once, got up to check on the kids at night. He was usually in a drunken stupor and snored like a chainsaw.'

He never woke up. Not even that night when Sara screamed and screamed for hours because she dreamed about those stupid cartoon creatures they have on that ad on TV, the ones that live under the rim of the toilet. She was sure she'd seen them for real, squirming out to get at her in all their horrible green yukkiness. Poor kid. Amazing it didn't wake him. She kept *me* awake all night and boy, was I pissed off with those stupid buggers who make the ads. She refused to use the toilet for weeks.

I'm better off now. At least I don't have the pain, the fear, the loneliness of having Joe living with me any more. Even though I am alone, I don't have to face the fact of having a partner who doesn't help anyway. That's as bad as having no one, except you have to stand by and watch them doing nothing when you need their help. He'd shout, 'Fuck off, you lazy bitch!' when I asked for help. Then he'd sit in front of the telly and drink beer, night after night — while I struggled along on too little sleep — then abuse me into the bargain. Well *I* can do without that and so can the kids.

She shrugged on her faded blue towelling dressing gown and shambled into Jamie's room. He was now quietly sobbing, or was it singing? His nappy-clad bum pointing up into the air, his face buried in his flat pillow.

'Good morning, darling,' Anne said, pulling back the curtains. Outside the early dawn sky was pink, the sun just beginning to rise. It isn't as *early* as I expected, thank goodness, she thought as she picked her little son up. She stripped off his wet nappies and dropped them in the washing machine.

'Mum, mum, mum,' sang Jamie as Anne rinsed him under a warm shower. Then she wrapped him in a towel and took him back to bed. Jamie snuggled in to her body and sucked his thumb contentedly, drifting off to sleep. She lay dreamily staring out the window. Another hour before the alarm will go off and I have to get up and get Sara ready for school.

I should have married a man who wanted kids. A man who was willing to truly share the housework and rearing the kids with me. Not someone who just expected me to do all the work like his mum had. If I'd had that kind of support then maybe I could have gone to cooking school and become a professional chef. She sighed — imagine that . . . inventing special dishes for special occasions.

Culinary creativity, one of the sexiest professions even if most people didn't see it like that.

She saw herself walking out through a crowded restaurant — *her* restaurant — holding an amazing dessert high above her head, covered in blue flames, or maybe crunchy golden caramel strands fluttering from the big white porcelain dish. The honoured guest was a warm, handsome foreigner with deep lustrous black hair and olive skin. He stood and thanked her for the special dessert with a kiss on each cheek and, once he had sat down, took her hand and passionately kissed the back of her knuckles, just like men did in old movies.

Ignoring the cooking aromas from her hot skin, looking up into her eyes, asking a silent question and she trembling at the desire she saw behind his question. She knew in that moment that her tawny, tanned beauty and the deliciousness of her cooking had won him, despite the blonde piece of fluff who sat at the table opposite him.

Sure enough, later in the evening he came to her kitchen, after the restaurant had closed and he had sent the blonde home alone. He stood leaning against the wall beside the cool-room talking to her while she prepared the basics for tomorrow. Then, her heart beating faster, she would dismiss the last dishwashers so they could be alone.

'A glass of my best wine?'

'Please.' Julio looked deep into her eyes as she handed

him the glass, glowing red in the bright kitchen lights. 'To you – sublime chefess extraordinaire,' he murmured in that gorgeous accent. Catching her hand and moving ardently closer to Anne, he seemed strong and sure of what he wanted. She drank in the smell of his body, a freshly pressed shirt, warm well-worn woollen suit, a vague hint of cologne. An indescribably delicate promise of all things masculine, the taste of orange in a sorbet, hints of pork in dripping, the bouquet of flowers in an excellent dessert liqueur.

Sipping her wine and breathing deeply she looked into her admirer's dark eyes as he leaned forward to place a long, supple, moist kiss on her lips. She melted, irradiated like soft butter in her microwave. His arms drew her into him and her wineglass shattered on the stone floor as his body pressed against her with an urgency she had never felt from a man before.

Warm, fragrant, opening up like a garlic clove in the heat of the oven she drank in Julio's exotic kisses. As if he were a divine liqueur poured over trifle, she absorbed all he had to give her. Starvation in the midst of plenty. Needy, yet giving of herself in her cooking every day, Anne needed a lover. A passionate lover is as necessary as food for the body. Now he was on her menu at last.

Kisses like his were out of the ordinary because she had never had kisses like this before. Slow gentle explorations of the sensitive inner planes of her mouth with his tongue.

Her lips trembling as she answered his probing questions with eager mews of delight. The taste of him so sweet, so pure, totally unlike the beer and cigarettes of the man she was used to. The taste of a healthy man who cared for his body and his woman. She relaxed into the delight of being discovered by him. His smooth hands with their supple sensitive fingers travelled unhindered all over her hot oven-scented body.

Slowly he undressed her and as he removed her long white apron, her jeans and t-shirt, her lace camisole and panties, all Anne could think of was how deliciously his hair waved around his brow, how hot his mouth was on her skin. She wanted to seduce him herself but allowed him to take charge of her, to lift her up onto the chill stainless steel of the bench where her buttocks clenched at the shock of the cold as he knelt between her thighs and began to lap and suck her inner lips.

She gasped with delight and pleasure. How amazing! That he would lick me like this! This has never happened to me before. I'd been expecting he would thrust into me immediately, that's what I have endured before, but no. This delicious alchemist of a man knows other things. Secrets like the sauces I cook, secrets about how to seduce a woman with a hundred different delicious methods. Just as I seduce tastebuds in a thousand subtle ways every day.

Julio licked and licked at Anne, now and then sending her into transports of delight by thrusting his fingers deep inside her. Moving them in such a way that she writhed, perched on the bench, her hands braced behind her, her legs braced apart on the chill steel. Her most sensitive sex wide and vulnerable yet feeling worshipped, adored. Pleasured as she had earlier delighted him with the especially delicious dessert she had made for him.

Almost – almost coming. Anne gasped and moaned *in extremis* – and he stopped. Stood up and kissed her, pulling her off the bench and against him. Unashamedly wanting him, wanting that climax, wanting Julio to continue to complete her pleasure, Anne pressed herself against his still-clothed body. Panting, she slid her hand down the front of his trousers, feeling his erection exciting and firm against her fingers. Eagerly she began to undo his zipper.

He gently stopped her. 'Not yet,' he whispered and handed her his warm coat. 'Put this on and wait there.' His look at her a pledge: 'I promise to pleasure you, to sex you, to cream you with my inner self, to fulfil that woman, that sensual cook, the lustful woman you are. I will, I am on my way.' Quickly Julio walked out into the restaurant and Anne heard the front door open and close, clicking softly in the way she knew so well.

A little chill grew on her skin as the kitchen cooled. The steamy warmth and delicious smells of the evening's catering were steadily being sucked from the air by humming ventilators. Cooling, yet wet and desiring, urgently needing her release, Anne stood waiting, not knowing what else to do. Where on earth had he gone? Was she doomed to be always let down by men? When her lover had been out of the kitchen for a couple of minutes she moved to the gas hob and put a kettle of water on to heat for coffee.

Lingering beside the leftovers from dinner Anne tasted a little of the coffee cream she had made for him and ahhh, it was divinely scented. Powered with alcohol and coffee with just a hint of cocoa. Her mouth watered, recognising ambrosia on the tongue.

She leaned back against the bench, desiring to surrender, to be taken by him, to climb heights of united sexual pleasure she had never shared before. Trembling because the feeling of fulfilment was so close, so very close.

Reaching for the dessert bowl again she thrust three fingers into the coffee cream and scooped a trembling glob into her hand. She studied the creamy beige mass for a few moments and then began to lick and suck it from her palm, feeling the touch of her tongue with a new awareness, the tingle of the tip as it passed over the fine lifelines of her palm. How sexy she felt as she slowly savoured the delicious dessert! Eating as she hadn't eaten since she was a small child: pushing handfuls of delicious food into her hungry mouth with her bunched, chubby fists.

Julio hurried through the kitchen door and it swung shut behind him with a bang. When he saw her eating from her palm with what was plainly sensual delight he moaned deep in his throat. 'Ahhh my beautiful sexy woman.' Anne noticed his suit sat taut over his groin and, much more mysterious, hanging from his strong fingers was a coil of thick rope which swung back and forth as he walked towards her.

'What are you doing?' she asked, as, obedient and trusting she allowed him to tie her hands behind her back. Her question wasn't answered except by a kiss. Julio took the bowl of coffee cream and scooped some out with his fingers. He tasted it, nodded his head in approval and pressed his fingers to Anne's lips. She surrendered to his insistent touch, opened her mouth and sucked greedily on them. How lovely to helplessly suck on his fingers! Anne felt more and more dependent and childlike. He took more cream and stroked it on her nipples, then sucked and licked it off them. She watched in fascination, wondering what he was going to do next and what all the rest of the rope was for.

Slowly, teasing her with his voice, Julio took off his clothes, revealing a lightly muscled firm body powdered with fine dark hairs which gathered in thickness and darkness at his groin. He was erect, his penis thrusting fat and slick towards her. Anne salivated, thinking of the touch of it against her lips. Julio took some more cream and anointed the glowing knob of his erection and motioned to Anne. She sank to her knees on the chill floor and began to suck him. Carefully licking off the alcoholic dessert and then surrounding his penis with her warm lips, savouring the taste of him, the sweet strong juice which began to seep from him, the soft moans he produced as she thrust her tongue under his beautiful glans and sucked on his foreskin folded there.

Anne's knees hadn't time to get tired or her mouth ache from sucking before Julio asked her to stand and he moved her over to the stainless steel table again. This time he bent her over it, tying her hands so she was standing almost on tip-toe, spread over it, the chill steel shocking her throbbing, hot body. She cried out with the cold but he took no notice of her protests, busily tying her ankles to the legs of the table so she was spread wide open for him.

Then she couldn't see what he was doing any more, and couldn't control what he was doing either. The helplessness of her position in her own kitchen with one of her most regular customers aroused Anne even more. She longed to thank him for this experience even though it hadn't finished, that is until she felt the chill as he ran an ice cube all over her bottom. She screamed and he began to spank her buttocks firmly so they stung and started to glow hot and red. Anne couldn't tell any more if she was hot or cold as her lover alternated the ice and the spanking until all of her glowed and tingled.

He began to caress her clitoris and massaged some of the ambrosial dessert all around her sex. Slowly, tantalisingly, he licked her clean again. She moaned and begged him to enter her; she was aroused more than she had ever experienced in her life. All he did was slip one slim finger into her and she sobbed with frustration.

Next he slid a finger into her ass and she stiffened with surprise. This was a different, more intense feeling, a feeling of fullness, of urgency, of a forbidden pleasure becoming available. A rare truffle placed on the dish of sex in front of her and offered, suggested, as a dainty morsel to try for size.

'Nn-nn-noooo!' Anne moaned. 'Oh please please fuck me. I'm ready, I want to come.'

'OK my darling, my sweet amour.' Her lover moved in between her thighs, slipped his erection into her and as he did so sang, 'My chérie amour, pretty little girl that I adore,' and Anne, irritated at his idiocy at singing just when his gorgeous cock was about to give her what she longed for, woke and discovered the song being played on the radio because it had turned on automatically at 6.55 am. Grumpily she turned the radio off and lay there, feeling almost as aroused as in her dream and wondering if she dared masturbate while Jamie lay asleep beside her.

Her body, deprived of satisfaction, ached and throbbed. She tossed and turned several times, longing to go back to the dream but the reality of morning, of Sara stirring in the next room and Jamie now awake and climbing out of bed, put paid to any more dreaming.

Chapter 5

ANTHROPOLOGY

'Are you at home about 3.30?' asked Lynne.

'Yes, I think so, unless I get held up at school with Sara. Do you want to come round for coffee? I haven't seen you for ages.'

'That was what I was thinking about — I have the afternoon off work today and I've got this amazing thing to tell you!' Anne smiled. Lynne was such a dreamer, almost as bad as she was.

'See you later then darling,' Anne hung up the phone. What new woman would Lynne have fallen in love with at the supermarket checkout? Or would she have seen long female legs at hockey practice and fallen in lust as she did at least once a week? Well, she'd find out later, Lynne couldn't keep a secret about her love-life for more than five minutes.

❧

'Hey! Look at this one!' Tina had a newspaper draped across her knee. She was making a flying lunchtime visit to Anne's cottage since she had been selling a property in that area. Her fingers moved down the columns of *Matchless Love*. ' "Financially secure 35-year-old executive with great sense of humour. Six feet tall, blond, blue-eyed, easy on the eye" – read 'vain' – "seeks to share life's adventures with fun-loving lady who enjoys romance, dining out, tramping and water sports." That could be you – eh?'

'Aw – nah. I don't really want an executive. They work too hard and anyway, he doesn't say anything about kids. I bet he isn't interested in kids.' Anne felt negative about ads in newspapers. 'Who has *ever* met anyone compatible through a newspaper ad? Tell me that?' she scrubbed the kitchen stove fiercely.

'Aw – I know at least one happy couple who got married a few months after they met through an ad. And – there's that dinner party for six thingy. You could book in for that. I know people who have done that a few times and met someone really great.'

'Yeah – but it all comes down to money. Always bloody money. I don't have enough money to buy petrol and keep the car going let alone to pay to go out to dinner with a bunch of people I don't know at all.'

'God! You're impossible – you know that? I don't know why I'm wasting my time with you!' Tina exclaimed, looking down at the paper again. 'Hey — listen to this one then: "Gorgeous male. Free to a good home. Will require training with a good reward system. Lies like a trooper, the worse for wear but loveable." Now *he* sounds like a challenge!'

Anne put down the scrubber and wiped her forehead with a hot hand. She sighed. 'I have enough challenges in my life with two kids. What would I want to give a stray liar a home for? If I want to have another kid who needs rewards and punishments, I'll get pregnant!'

'Yeah, I suppose you're right,' conceded Tina, looking down the columns. She giggled. 'What about this one then? "Arrest me! My crime — 6'2" policeman, outgoing, sporty, charged with wicked sense of humour. Presently in solitary confinement. Seeks bail from spunky woman who likes sports, gym, dining out, social drinking. For friendship, poss relationship." Now I have no objections to going out with a policeman — what about you? That is such a *cute* ad! I feel like replying to it myself.'

'Well go ahead then.' Anne was unimpressed. 'I don't want a guy who has the weird hours and stresses that policemen get. My life is full enough of stress as it is with two kids, without having my man out all hours and on call other times. Anyhow, I'm not like you, I'm not into gym and tramping. The last time, the *only* time I went tramping, was when I was at a school camp and it nearly killed me. I hated it – being forced to almost run for twelve miles of solid bush and freezing scree-covered mountain is *not* my idea of fun.'

She pouted. 'Forget it, Tina. Find some other way to introduce me to men, please.'

Lynne arrived soon after Anne got home from school with Sara and Jamie. Anne made them all pikelets while Lynne sat at the kitchen table and talked, sipping a dry white wine she had brought to share with Anne. 'Oh Nadia was soooo gorgeous, Anne. You are too straight to see women as attractive, I know, but really! She was fantastic, a butch-looking blonde lawyer. Probably het too . . . more's the pity.' She sighed despondently. 'I desperately *need* a woman in my life, Anne. It's been too long since Ros and I split up. Mind you, I'm also incredibly horny today because I had this amazing sexual dream last night – wanna hear it?'

Anne grinned, looked at Lynne and sipped her wine. Did she have the option of saying no? Not really, Lynne would tell her anyhow. She dropped spoonfuls of pikelet mix into the frying pan and buttered the cooked hot pikelets, putting them on a big plate piled high and steaming in the centre of the table. Jamie was munching on two pikelets, one gripped squidgily in each fist, dripping strawberry jam all over himself and the floor.

'Surprise me,' said Anne as she took a hot buttery

pikelet and bit into it, savouring the sweet and salty soft texture of the hot cake.

'I dreamed that I was part of this experimental group of anthropologists who all specialised in monkey behaviour. We were locked up in a building complex supplied with vegetarian food and basic toilet and washing facilities. A bit like those weirdo made-on-the-cheap TV programmes that give the big prize to the one who goes nuts in the empty room or on the desert island last. Lots of warm carpeted rooms, exercise spaces, no clothes on any of us. There were about 27 women and 19 men, of all ages, plus a couple of breast-feeding mothers and babies.

'We were experimenting with living in a group like chimps or bonobo monkeys. Trying out what their lifestyle is like: gathering food, having sex, being social all the time, not just some of the time like we are. Ignoring all the social and work taboos that have us in a straitjacket every day. Trying to use the social structures that have been observed in various species of monkeys and seeing if we humans could use them too.

'Some of the men were bored, of course. Couldn't cope with the social lifestyle; they missed their machines and sports and their other things to play with. But we just noted their responses and kept on playing and talking and preening each other. It was a marvellously intimate experience, you know? That was the main feeling of the dream, a deep warm intimacy and sharing. Being human together using an ancient formula which we haven't altogether forgotten.

'I felt *so* close to the women. Of course we all began menstruating and ovulating together but the best thing was — the men were only allowed to have sex with us when we were ovulating! You have *no* idea how freeing that is, to know you can have sex with whoever you wanted only on about three or four days a month. Those poor guys, how tired they were! They needed a good long rest when we'd finished with them!' Anne looked at her friend with her eyebrows raised. She hadn't expected Lynne, a lesbian most of her life, to admit to the possibility that men could feature usefully in a woman's sex life.

'Yeah, yeah, I know, this was a *dream* remember, not reality and the main thrill of my dream was when we women got together spontaneously, without any discussion — and masturbated. All in a big circle, opening up our lovely frilly or tulip-shaped cunts and stimulating ourselves as a group. Breasts and thighs rubbing together, sighs and moans of pleasure. Lots of cuddles and kisses and long, slow, teasing touches. Oh it was so intimate, so yummy and sexy!

'The men gathered together and watched us, their cocks all erect and unashamed. We women ignored them, we were too busy watching each other, as, whispering, giggling, touching, each of us orgasmed. It was a wild space, with the women's orgasms happening at different times, in so many different ways. I loved the feeling of closeness, of community that we achieved together as women.

'I had this special partner, she was a luscious tall blonde. We had such strong gorgeous erotic times together as part of that group. Sometimes we'd tribade, you know, rub our aroused wet slippery cunts together, our mouths meeting and our nipples rubbing across the other's nipples . . . rubbing and rubbing, sometimes hard, other times soft and gentle . . . ohhhh . . .' She sighed and wriggled in her seat. 'I haven't had a wet dream like that in ever so long. It was so powerful, I came in the middle of it.'

Lynne laughed, delighted with herself. 'Those apes have a really lovely time, you know. The females play with their clits a lot and no one hassles them about it. It's just a part of being alive for them, making their own pleasure and feeling free to do it. A bit like men and how they play with themselves.' Lynne went to her bag and drew out a small cloth bundle.

'You must be getting pretty frustrated Anne, after all this time with no sex.' She sounded concerned, 'What about a woman in your life? There's plenty around who could give you a good time.'

Anne laughed at her. 'Oh come on, Lynne! How long have we been friends? Ten years or so? If I was a lesbian or bi – well you'd know it by now, surely! I won't rule out the possibility of a woman in my life altogether. The idea of having someone who could cook and help with the dishes and the kids sounds like heaven on a stick. But really, it's not going to happen. You and Tina are always trying to get me set up with someone!

'You're as bad as mum, Michelle and Kate when it comes to trying to find me a partner. Everyone seems to think I *need* someone, and their responsibility is to find that person for me.

'Hell! — I'm still recovering from Joe and what he did to me. I'm probably a liability instead of an asset to anyone just at the moment. And Tina! She's the worst of the lot, she even brought a paper around today and read out dozens of ads from lonely men looking for relationships!'

'Did she really?' Lynne was laughing.

'Yes!' Anne was attempting grumpiness. 'I really don't know how to have a successful relationship. I really have *no* idea what to do or where to start.' She poured the herb tea into cups and looked at Lynne seriously, almost dissolving into tears. 'I met Joe and spent eight years with him. I haven't had any other boyfriends — *ever*. If other men aren't abusive like him it will be a welcome relief to me, but since I've never had a relationship with anyone else it's really hard for me to visualise myself having anything different from what I got from Joe and I can tell you now — that's a really big stumbling-block for me. There is no way I want another abusive relationship.'

Lynne reached out and touched Anne's hand gently, soothingly. 'I've had the same problems, you know,' she said softly. 'When I came out, first of all I had no idea how to have a relationship with a woman. What it would be like, who would do the dishes, make the bed, fold the washing. Sharing the work was a huge headache — hell it was all a totally new ball-game and I can only tell you one thing . . .' she paused, looked at Anne, and smiled. Anne smiled weakly back.

'What?'

'That any relationship is a blank book. Until you start into it and find out just who fits what role and when and — it changes all the time. Nothing is set in concrete any more.

'Once upon a time roles may have been fixed but now . . . well who knows? There are women who behave like men; they ride huge motorcycles and insist on mowing the lawns or fixing the car. Then there are men who manicure their nails and visit the beautician more often than you or I would, ever. They wax their legs and do the ironing without being asked. How can you make any assumptions when faced with all this flexibility among us?'

Anne frowned and then smiled. 'I . . . I suppose you are right. I hadn't thought about it that way before. I feel like a 25-year-old virgin, really. I'm just so aware I have *no* experience of a healthy relationship and I'm scared I won't even be able to recognise one even if I had it!'

'We're all in the same boat there, Anne. You don't know until you know. End of story. It's like when a couple meet and marry three weeks later. Some couples who do that end up married forever — success stories if you like. If that really *is* how you measure success; and others split after varying lengths of time, but — does that make those relationships failures?

'Length of time together means nothing except that you have learnt some more things, travelled down a path in life. *No one* can tell us if the person we meet tomorrow and fall in love with is the right one who will give us the other half of a lifelong partnership. And — hell! I have to ask myself — do I *really* want the "unto death do us part" thing?'

Anne laughed and scrubbed her hands over her face. 'Yes, I know what you mean. I don't know about that any more either. I don't *think* I want marriage again, at least not for a long time. Marriage has been tainted for me by what happened with Joe and I'd have to be really super-sure the same thing wasn't going to repeat on me before I looked at committing to a long-term relationship with anyone, no matter how much I loved them.'

'Well marriage has always been tainted for me, and *I've* never been married!' Lynne laughed and stood up. 'Come on, let's read your tarot cards, I bet they'll say you will meet a tall dark stranger and live happily ever after . . . Not!'

'OK,' said Anne, laughing too. 'Then we'll take the kids for a walk down to the river before dinner.'

Chapter 6

S P U D S

Anne idly peeled the potatoes, skimming off the thin brown skins into the sink, rinsing the smooth flesh under the chill water from the cold tap, slicing the crisp white flesh into uneven chunks and pouring them into the saucepan full of hot water on the stove. Trying to avoid the splashes, enjoying the dangerous game she was having with herself. Avoiding the knife, the scalding water. Relishing the challenge of cooking dinner so as to have it all ready to eat at once.

Relationships: men and women, women and women, men and men, whirled around in her brain in an unending merry-go-round of ideals and ideas. What would be best for her? Was the tarot reading right? Would she meet a man and a woman and fall in love with them both? Nah — that was just too preposterous!

Should she try placing an ad in the contact pages?

What about answering a few promising-looking ads like Tina suggested? She shivered, thinking of the scariness of sticking her neck out so far. But despite the fear she *did* want to meet someone new. Yes.

Why should Joe ruin her life and force her into a celibacy created by fear? No way was she going to let that happen.

Suddenly she saw a male vision in her mind's desiring eye. A stranger — yet real, and so *familiar*. A blonde youth with long tumbled curls was kneeling at her feet. He looked adoringly up at her, then leaned down and kissed her grotty old sneakers. Maybe the idea of owning love slaves had originated in one of those romantic legends from medieval times. She used to read them a lot when she was a teenager. Romances about having a handsome male servant to love; or a servant in love with her. A slave sometimes, in some of those Roman Empire romances. Yet exalted in his service to her. Paid only by love. Love of her being all the food and drink he wished for. All he lived for was her pleasure and her anger was death to him.

A man who would kneel at her feet, whenever and wherever she wanted. A good-looking cheeky guy who smiled and laughed, had a steady job but wanted, nay needed, to submit to her will. An ordinary bloke but her personal slave.

So when she said proudly to her friends, 'My man will do what I say,' she knew in full confidence that this was so. That any need, want, whim, order, requirement she would have of him would be obeyed, fulfilled, acted upon, met, adored and worshipped because serving her was the sole object of his life.

Just thinking of having a man in her life like this made Anne suddenly feel faint, weak at the knees. She leaned against the bench, swaying as if drunk. Drunk with a sudden alcoholic attack of desire. She took a deep breath, tried to centre herself. Hell, did – could – such a man exist?

Was there one whom she could trust to kiss her until she tired of kisses, only to place him tenderly between her thighs and have him service her clit until she came and came again? Could there be a man whose cock would rise and fall at her requirement? Never in the days of her period, perhaps; and then twice, three times a day when she really needed sex. Ready whenever she wanted him. What an intoxicating thought. What a divine thought!

She saw him, kneeling at her feet, looking up at her in adoration, in expectation and she slumped back. Sat in a chair beside the kitchen table, gazing sightlessly at the chaos left by the children; everything needed tidying before they could eat their dinner. Anne took a shuddering breath, then let it out, took another breath and slowly relaxed.

She felt full of an exhilaration she couldn't remember feeling before. A kind of megalomania, maybe. Like the feeling of standing on the summit of Mt Everest without knowing how you got there. Discovery of a new-found land within herself. Captainess Cook sailing into the great Southern Ocean of her inner heroine without a map, merely a hunch about what she was looking for and here, now, while peeling the spuds she had found him. The outline of the shape of a significant other.

So if having a man subservient to her was indeed the answer, well what then? How to find such a creature? Did she deserve to have a man who served her, who adored her with the look such as she saw in the eyes of her vision of a slave kneeling at her feet?

Wasn't this just a medieval fantasy? Men worshipping women! She snorted to herself, they certainly don't exist around here. Anne sighed longingly, thinking that after the incessant illogical demands of Joe, a man who simply demanded to serve her lovingly in the best way he knew how would be such a relief.

She could relax into his love and trust him completely and he would trust her to tell him what she wanted. Do what she needed, help her and support her, encourage her and assist her. Help to parent her kids instead of undermining her motherhood.

'Ooooooooooo . . .' she sighed. 'Oh if only . . .' In the out breath of her yearning she imagined a glorious muscular male body lying on her four-poster bed, face up – his penis raised in supplication. She snapped the manacles attached to each corner of the bed around his wrists and ankles, padlocking them securely. His beautiful body was now spreadeagled, open and helpless before her.

'You have been a disobedient boy,' she heard herself say sternly. 'You will stay here all day until you repent fully of your disobedience.' She swept out of the room in her long red dress which laced at the front, falling in fullness to the floor and trailing out behind her.

She felt like a queen as she left the room, so she had her other slaves massage her and bathe her until she knew the manacled slave was ready for her attention.

Of course she found him just as she had left him, looking at her with dark, longing, loving eyes. A gag forcing his mouth open wide. His penis still erect and weeping onto the silken skin of his belly. Slowly Anne disrobed. Unlacing the dress she let it fall to the floor. Beneath it she had on a black lace corset, garter belt and stockings. She checked the red stiletto high heels she had worn all day and got up on the bed. She stood over him, teetering on one red high heel as she rested her other steel-shod foot on his chest. She steadied herself on the canopy of the four-poster.

'Are you sorry for your mistakes?' she demanded of him. He nodded vigorously, murmuring something around the ball of the gag. Anne knelt, then slowly smoothed her nose and lips over his smooth, shaven flanks, up to his armpits and down to his groin, back to his nape and over his lips cruelly distended by the gag.

She then gently ran her lips over the satin skin of his penis, even more erect now that her almost nude body was near him. She gently licked the juices which had slowly leaked from him onto his belly. He moaned softly. Anne moved her mouth up to his nipples. She swiftly bit down onto the sensitive flesh of his breast and he cried out sharply around the gag, his body convulsing in the restraints, bucking against the bed.

She watched until his pain had subsided and then brushed her own very acutely sensitive nipples over his, feeling the tingles of his pain sparkling through her like champagne. Her eyes glowing, lips smiling wickedly.

Knowing how much he enjoyed their regular Sunday sessions together. Laughing inside at how he was her boyfriend every day, visiting almost every night. He lived just down the road — everyone knew they were lovers but not *this* kind of lover. This was their special secret. Every Sunday they travelled in time to this medieval bedroom, lit by candles, the four-poster decorated with deep red curtains, pulleys and hooks, chains and ropes. For these weekly celebrations of servitude, love and pain. Their own private, wholly delicious secret.

She knelt between his legs, stroked his balls and then drew a wide red ribbon out of her corset and tied each testicle up as a tight separate package. He sighed and arched his back at her. Anne then lubed her fingers and slipped them into him, slowly delving, moving gently but firmly. Knowing how much he enjoyed her touch anywhere and everywhere on and in his body. Knowing his intense love and gratitude were cascading over her even in the silence enforced by the gag.

Aroused by his helplessness and his trust, his lovely sexy compliant body, she bestrode him and removed the gag. He licked his lips. 'Thank you, mistress,' he whispered.

Anne crouched, straddling his face, lowered her weeping cunt onto his lips. 'Lick me well, slave,' she ordered. Warning him with her tone not to do more than pleasure her as he knew so well how to do. Not to take liberties, the man living in a glass house . . . The slave tied up has no choices, can decide nothing, say nothing without permission, do nothing without a command. I can relax and order what I want when I want it and lo . . . it arrives, presented on a plate with love and oh!

His tongue began a slow wet sensual dance around her clit, and Anne allowed herself to slide down into the deep bright whirlpool of pleasure and delight he created in her body. Sparkling shivers shafting through her like electrical shorts in a microwave. Her breath coming in gasps of delight, toes curling, nipples erect, she leaned forward, supporting herself on all fours as he continued to suck and lick her, mouthing her most sensitive spots. As Anne grew closer to coming she felt barely able to hold onto her consciousness but with a huge effort of will gathered herself together and changed position. Spread her labia open around his penis and sank onto him. Her deep cry of satisfaction met his cry of completion as she took him, rode him to pleasure and pleasure again and yet again.

When she found the strength to move she unlocked the manacles. Setting him free to wrap his arms around her and hold her, kissing her cheeks, her lips, her eyes and brows over and over. Whispering, 'I love my mistress. Thank you, mistress,' until she slept smiling, her head cradled on his shoulder.

'Mum! Mum!' Sara ran into the room shouting, holding her muddy hands outstretched. Anne shook herself and shuddered as she beheld the chubby hands of her daughter filled with pink earthworms squirming in black humus which she was dripping all over the floor. 'Grandma says we can make a worm farm with these. Can we? Oh can we please? Mum?'

'Yes darling, what a good idea. We can feed them our compost bucket, can't we?' Anne stood up, a little dazed.

'Good grief, Anne, what's burning?' Mum had come in with Jamie on her hip and hurried over to the stove to check it. 'You've boiled the spuds dry! I thought you were making dinner for us? Burnt spuds aren't your usual offering.' Her mother was looking hard at her. Anne blushed bright and hot, she could feel it on her cheeks. Her mother was laughing at her. 'What a silly mummy you have Jamie,' said grandma to her grandson. 'We're going to go hungry tonight if your mum doesn't stop daydreaming about men, or whatever it is she's been thinking and blushing about.'

Suddenly Anne had the strongest feeling the love scene she had dreamed was just a fantasy. Nothing that could or would ever happen for her, for her own pleasure. She was just a solo mum who burned the spuds. Not a princess with a slave to serve her every urge; to tie up and torture, take her pleasure with and then leave him as the impulse took her.

'Sorry mum,' she said, 'I *have* been daydreaming.' So she began all over again, peeling a new batch of spuds while her mother played with the kids, making a worm farm. The pot of burned potatoes steamed and smoked out in the garden, like the frustration simmering in her body, wetting her panties.

Chapter 7

LADIES' NIGHT

'Hey girl! There's a ladies' night on downtown in the pub. Wanna go?'

Anne sighed; Tina was trying to get her out on the town again. 'You *know* that I can't get time off, Tina. I could ask mum if she'll come round and look after the kids for the evening but she's working this week. Why would I want to go to a ladies' night anyway? What would it do for me?'

'Awwww . . . well.' Tina seemed to be inventing a good reason, 'I know you haven't got a lot of experience of men and it'll be an opportunity for you to get a good look at some spunky naked blokes. Hell, it might turn you on to men again. It's been a whole year and a bit now, hasn't it? You've had enough time to get over Joe, surely.' Tina was wheedling now. 'I'll talk to your mum, ask her myself eh?'

Anne groaned, imagining Tina persuading her weary

mum to look after her kids one just more time.

'If your mum agrees to babysit will you come with me?'

'OK, I'll come. But only if you shout me. I haven't got any money at all. I don't even know how I'm going to keep Sara at school, I'm that short of cash.'

'OK, OK, I'll shout you too. I really want you to come with me, I need the company. So I'll phone your mum now, right?' Tina sounded delighted. Anne was smiling in resignation; just as well Tina had a good job and could afford to take her out.

❧

Anne and Tina lined up with dozens of women outside the pub, waiting to get inside to see the show. Anne felt nervous and slightly embarrassed at the thought of seeing nude men, or almost nude. She suspected that when it came down to it she wouldn't get to see any cocks. No lovely erect penises on display.

She had loved Joe's cock. Sometimes when he was asleep she would gently reach over and hold it as he slept. She loved the silken feel of that special skin, so different from the rest of his body. She loved the beauty of Jamie's tiny erection too. Anne blushed and looked at her tatty trainer-clad toes.

Tina was babbling on about the men in the programme. 'I saw that one, calls himself Gary, last year. He's a real spunk. You'll think so too, Anne, I promise you.' Anne looked absently at the photograph of the glossy, muscular, grinning strippers. She thought of her mum, back at the cottage, reading the kids a goodnight story. It felt entirely too wicked, like she was shirking her duty as a mother, standing here waiting in line to watch a bunch of blokes strip their clothes off for the enjoyment of women.

She shivered, rubbing her cold hands up and down her upper arms to try to warm them. It was embarrassing to think that she'd only ever seen one nude man in her whole life and there was *no* chance that Joe would ever have stripped sexily for her enjoyment. His idea of alluring was to sniff his armpits and growl inarticulately before grabbing her and pushing her down on the bed.

Ann thought about the strippers; they *must* be different. Maybe they were blokes who liked women, who wanted to show off for women and give them the gift of a fit, muscular, rippling body, an enthusiastic smile. Give back to women the possibility of having a lustful desire for men when most of them were used to their men dressed in checked bush shirts, ripped jeans and underpants full of holes. Oil-soaked overalls, grubby jerseys and beer-flabbed bellies were what a lot of these women were going home to later tonight. Lucky me, thought Anne. Just a safe cosy empty bed to climb into and the kids again in the morning. She sighed.

Tina looked relaxed. Chewing gum, hanging out in her high heels, fishnet tights, leather miniskirt and crop top. She looked rather stunning. 'Why are you dressed like that?' asked Anne when Tina picked her up. 'I'm OK in jeans and this top, aren't I?'

'Yeah, course you are! I have *plans*,' Tina said determinedly. 'My main aim is to get laid tonight.' She grinned as she drove them into town and parked near the pub, refusing to answer any of Anne's questions. She had a heavy leather handbag which she plonked on the ground at her feet with a clank.

Inside the pub the women were drinking. Some were having more than a few. Almost everyone was talking loudly, preening, highly excited. There were odd couples who stood around quietly, not looking the part. Middle-aged girlfriends just waiting for the show, Anne thought. It took an hour of drinking to get the women warmed up until at 8 pm the organisers turned all the lights out for ten minutes or so.

By the time the act started Anne was almost *dying* of excitement. She rubbed her hands together but the chill wouldn't go away from her nervous skin. Tina turned and smiled at her friend, her lips glistening and her teeth a greenish white in the exit light – then she suddenly leaned over and kissed Anne on the cheek and laughed, exhilarated.

'Thanks for keeping me company, Anne,' she said. 'I was a bit nervous about tonight.' It seemed like all the audience were laughing, breathing deeply, anticipating the men, the sex, the clothes — the excitement, the fulfilling of a fantasy of lovely sexy muscular young men performing for *us*, just for women. Instead of us performing for men.

The first guy to leap onto the stage was dressed as a matador, swinging his cloak, with music which started out in a boring classical style. As the music gradually hyped up he paraded up and down with two other guys in leotards gyrating their bodies beside him. Gradually he began moving faster, spinning on his high Spanish boot heels. It seemed to Anne that his clothes began slowly and then swiftly to move, to leave his body, as the music got louder and more and more heavy and modern. By this time he was down to his rippling glossy muscles and G-string; tantalising us, having us on, grinning with those lovely white teeth as if we were piano keys and he was playing us. Our acreage rising and falling with his presence, his closeness to us, that sweet mysterious bulge in his groin — at the last Anne and Tina were screaming and holding hands, pressing thighs vibrating to the male.

Pumped up with the music and the sight of a perfect male body rutting, showing off, shamelessly strutting his sexual self and loving us. It was his love that had us loving him. The smell of sex was in the air as he ran down into the audience. A contrast to the women seated there, with his slick brown skin, long dark curled hair and stripped muscles. He reappeared having picked up a woman out of

76

her chair. We gasped as he carried her in his arms up onto the stage. He was talking to her, we couldn't hear his words but when he set her down she stood behind him and began to run her hands all over him while he undulated and purred all round her. She seemed to be almost fainting from happiness and embarrassment. As Anne watched the woman violate 'Aaron's' perfect spotlit body with her hands she could feel the energy of all the other women around her, radiating: 'I wish *I* could be up there in her place. I'd do that better than *her*. Ohhhhh now if it was *me* . . . I'd *die* if that was me . . .'

Anne's body vibrated to her core, she'd never been this turned on before. She longed for and simultaneously dreaded the possibility that one of the strippers would choose her and carry her up on stage. Everyone would see her dull scrappy hair and tatty gym shoes then. But she wouldn't care. She'd get to touch him, smell him, talk to him and hear his voice. Just the thought of it made her tremble uncontrollably.

As each man did his performance – riding in on a Harley, pretending to be a private detective or Clark Gable, acting out every romantic fantasy Anne had ever had and more – she became more and more aroused, restless, feeling nervous, out of control. Jailed by her circumstances. She secretly wished that she could 'get laid' tonight like Tina. But *what* was Tina going to do to get her man? She shuddered to think.

During the interval Tina sat beside Anne, sipping wine. 'Anne,' she said thoughtfully. 'You'll have to take my car home. Don't worry about me, I'll get a taxi.'

'Why? Aren't you coming home with me?' asked Anne, wishing she had the same autonomy. The show was running later than she had expected and she had promised her mother to be home by 11 at the latest. This was worse than being a teenager, being a mother responsible for little kids. Tina shook her head and grinned, shifting her heavy bag further under her seat.

Anne took a gulp of wine and shifted uneasily in the hard chair. Her body tingled from the accumulated sight and sound of men, men and more men. Plus the tension, the hot sexual tension of a big room full of sexually aroused women. You could *smell* the lust radiating from their bodies. What must it be like for those men up on stage, parading around, the focus of all this sexual desire?

'No. I've seen who I want and I'm going to have him. Tonight. Soooo . . .' Tina paused, then grinned. 'I don't think I'll be done with him before you have to be home for the kids. I *know* I won't be finished by then. We may not have even *begun*.'

'Is it – Gary?' asked Anne tentatively. He had been on twice in the first half and she remembered his stocky muscular body clearly. Especially when he had ridden onto the stage in the saddle of a huge black and silver Harley. Wooah! Did he know how to strut his stuff?

'Yeahhhh,' said Tina with a low sigh of satisfaction. 'I want him and I know just *what* he likes.' She sounded intense and husky.

Anne was bewildered. 'He was very sexy but — how do you know you can have him? Won't there be other women who want him too?'

'Oh yes. Heaps probably. But that won't stop me,' said Tina, leaning back in her chair and stretching. 'Oh God! I'm *so* horny — aren't you?'

Anne blushed. 'Yes, I suppose I am,' she admitted reluctantly. 'But I wouldn't want one of those strippers — no way! They must have dozens of women every week. I wouldn't want a guy like that!'

'Depends on what you want him *for*,' Tina said with a wolfish grin. 'I want Gary for sex — the way *I* want it.' She sipped her drink. 'I'm going to get it too, I can just about taste it.' She looked longingly in the direction of the stage. No, Tina, she told herself, *now* is not the time to go man-hunting. But after the show guess who will be elbowing her way backstage? The lights dimmed, the music pumped up the volume of a rock'n'roll rhythm and 'Dwight' leaped into the spotlight dressed as Lawrence of Arabia.

Anne watched, her fingers pressed deep between her thighs. She gently rocked back and forth to the beat of the music, the strides of the stripper's body, the lights strobing through the audience. Exquisite sensations ran through her body. She felt awake, alive for the first time in years. Ecstatic without being able to say why — just that she was enjoying every moment of this show; and as Lawrence of Arabia slid off his many robes, unveiling his polished exquisite body, she allowed her fingers to press deeper into her crotch.

Compressing and rocking where it felt the best. She was intently concentrating and as Lawrence finally gyrated his hips and flicked his G-string from his taut buttocks her body convulsed around her fingers and she leaned forward, panting and gasping, trying to hide her orgasm from Tina and the other women around them. They were roaring for more of the desert lover and his lovely body as he ran, robes held modestly in front of his groin, off the stage. He was immediately replaced by a reggae beat and 'Sir Michael', a tall black man with dreadlocks and wearing skintight leathers covered with zips which he slowly began to unzip with maximum effect on the audience.

❦

Tina lined up with all the other sweaty, gossiping women. Laughing, elbowing, hot excited female bodies jostling eagerly to get at, or at least get near, the gorgeous oiled strippers who were cramped in a network of tiny rooms out the back of the stage. Waiting and looking, pushing and shoving though the crowd which was very dense around 'Sir Michael' with the dreadlocks, eventually Tina managed to find Gary's dressing room. Undressing room would have been more accurate.

He was naked and stiff, almost vibrating. Standing in the middle of the room with his legs braced and eyes shut as a lovely brunette sucked eagerly on his erection. Tina didn't mind finding him like this. She imagined that all the other men were getting similarly serviced and she had expected that other women would have got to Gary before she did.

She was willing to wait. Tina watched the ecstasy on Gary's face slowly change to a kind of boredom with the woman's technique and eventually he said, 'That's enough, darling.' Wrapped a towel around himself and pushed her out the door. She left without complaint, a smug look on her face. Immediately another woman from outside, a big blousy blonde, shoved into the room, wrapped her arms and big bosom around the stripper's body and plastered his face with pale-pink lipsticked kisses.

'You were *wonderful* dahling!' she cried.

'Thanks – I know I was,' said Gary. 'Come back tomorrow night.' He handed her a free pass to the next show. 'Bring a girlfriend along too,' he added as he guided her firmly to the door. She ambled off down the hallway and Gary looked out. The crowds seemed to have dissipated. Sounds of moaning and panting were coming from most of the dressing rooms as was usual after a show.

He grinned, then an older woman hurried up and gushed, 'Oh Gary! You remind me of my son. You

81

gorgeous thing.' She hugged him, smothering him in a maternal embrace which reeked of gallons of 'Red Door'. He staggered back into the room after she had gone, glanced at Tina, and locked the door.

Tina grinned at him. She gleamed all over now she was locked in this tiny dressing room with this especially tasty hunk of extrovert manhood. Was she feeling like a Great White or what? She reached into her handbag and brought out her precious pair of US Police-issue handcuffs. The keys dangled from the lock.

Gary's erection was back in a few moments. He thrust the towel off his waist and eagerly held out his hands. In seconds Tina snapped the cold steel around his wrists. As she clicked the chill metal shut she said with satisfaction, 'There, now you're all *mine*.' Her final word almost hissed as if a demonic snake had possessed her and was finally finding a voice. She gently guided Gary to the centre of the room and ordered him to stand with his legs wide apart.

He trembled as Tina walked around his nude erect body. Sweat began to bedew his back as he thought that now, at last, a woman had him at *her* mercy. How he hated having to be in control of all the women who barged through the doors of his dressing rooms on their tour around the country. Having to say yes, or, much more frequently, no, when really all he had ever wanted to say was, 'Yes, mistress,' to one strong woman. 'Yes, mistress,' and kneel at her feet and let her do what she wanted to him. He would do whatever she wanted, now and forever.

As Tina began to stroke her captive slave all over with her fingers and then gently bite him across his back and chest she whispered, 'I first saw you a year ago, you gorgeous submissive. I could tell from a mile away that you were a sub. Your act hides nothing from me. I know you want me, were looking for me and now here I am. I am going to take you in all the ways that please me. Fuck you or not, just as I want and you will do just as I tell you.' She looked him in the eyes, her own gleaming with an inner fire that burned into his and he sighed deeply.

'Yes, mistress,' he said fervently for the first time in his life.

Tina smiled widely and slowly began to strip for Gary, putting every ounce of her energy into entertaining the stripper in her own way, arousing him as he had aroused her earlier in the evening. Undulating her body, bringing her breasts up close to him, her long blonde hair caressing his shoulders and face.

When she was down to her bra and panties she ordered Gary to kneel in front of her. He did, his eyes firmly anchored to her bright red stiletto-heeled boots. Then his gaze travelled slowly up her slim legs clad in the black fishnet stockings to the black suspender belt snapped to the stocking tops, emphasising the silken white flesh of her upper thighs. Her black lycra panties glistened over her mons – blonde hairs gleaming around the elastic lace trim of the panties. Gary sighed deeply and his erection began to spurt.

A loud knock rattled the door and then rough hands tried to open it. When it didn't budge a loud voice shouted, 'Gary! Come on mate! We're off out to the club.'

'OK,' shouted Gary from his knees. 'I'll be with you later.' There was no note of regret in his voice.

'Gotta good one eh?' speculated the voice, retreating. Loud laughter from the other men echoed down the hall as Tina grabbed Gary by the hair and pushed his face into her crotch. 'Mmmmmm,' he moaned happily as she ground her wet panties into his face.

Soon Tina sat on the make-up bench. She had slipped a chain collar around Gary's neck and padlocked a leash to it.

'Gary, slip my panties down my legs and take them off me.' He crawled to her, a look of complete happiness on his face as he slipped down her panties and gazed up at her. She smiled at him, thinking how much sweeter, more handsome, altogether more attractive he was kneeling at her feet than on stage. Breathtaking in fact.

'Now put my panties on over your cock.' Gary hurried to put on her tiny but very elastic panties. They didn't cover much of him at all but they looked good, swelling out, full of his balls. With his lovely erect cock thrusting out the top Tina thought he looked good enough to eat.

He knelt at her feet again and Tina ordered, 'Now eat me out, slave.'

The stripper moved close to her and with the handcuffs clinking against each other, began to part her lovely firm labia with his fingers. Reverently, gently, opening her sex like a secret flower that only he could access. He began to tongue her, to suck on her as he would suck the juice from a feijoa or a dripping ripe fig. Then he took long licks of her sweet wetness, tasting her evening of excitement, her longing for him, her desire for sex mingled with anxiety, uncertainty, the taste of determination.

Gary knew how long Tina had waited to get close to him, how many women he had had that day and that none had aroused him as she did. None had asked him to pleasure them like this, and, best of all, Gary liked to be told what to do and wanted to please only strong demanding women like Tina.

She lay back, the half-dozen light bulbs around the mirror behind her the only illumination. They were those wimpy power-saving variety so she was lit by a wan white glow and Gary's curls seemed frosted with fluorescence as he served her. How clever his tongue, how delightful his mouth on her receptive and vulnerable cunt. Her juices dripped into his mouth and he drank them eagerly, just as she wanted her body to drink his come.

By giving him her juices she was reversing that age-old

natural habit of men to give, always give their juices to women. Give their seed to make children, to create love. How strange that this special form of giving, this universal yet always unique communion of bodies, has been transformed by men into an act not of giving but of violence, of fear, of hurt. Brutality and punishment as well as pleasure, delight and love.

The receptivity of women is not seen as powerful, but as selfish taking or a vulnerability to be taken advantage of. Tina sighed. She knew that the giving and taking between men and women was more than this. Sacred when religion ceased to matter, essential beyond petty material concerns like money or possessions. Vital to keep us humans going and yet because of all these things used, abused, denigrated, feared and, for many, an unspoken activity full of secrecy, guilt and need.

'Ahhhh . . . I need you Gary,' she whispered as his tongue kept on and on stroking, caressing; building the feelings up in her body until she began to slip down the aquaslide of her orgasm, falling and falling, her body arched, ecstatic, swimming, flowing, brimming, plunging down and down until she submerged utterly. Gary on his aching knees, his mouth anchored to her, drinking her, overwhelmed with the power of her orgasm. Awed by this unique woman. There had been so many who had totally underwhelmed him. He shuddered in delight at pleasing his mistress.

Tina rested after her peak, panting as she surfaced to the reality of Gary still kneeling, handcuffed before her. She opened her bag and brought out a leather flogging whip. She bent Gary over the bench and began to hit him on his gorgeous tight ass. Slap, slap, slap with the flogger. 'Please — don't mark me mistress,' he begged, even as he loved the feeling of the strokes firm against his skin, warming him, giving a glow, a liveliness where formerly there had been none.

'Can't have a stripper with bruises and red marks on his skin now can we?' said Tina, grinning. 'It might show off just what a kinky boy he really is, now wouldn't it?' Knowing the fear of her harming him was adding to his experience. Gary sighed and surrendered to her as the punishment relaxed the tension in his body. Then Tina roped his wrists to the table, slipped on a latex glove, lubricated her fingers and slid one inside Gary as he lay, lit by the bulbs, reflected in the mirror.

He gasped and moaned, 'Oh yes!' as she gently thrust into him, his erection fuller and harder than ever. Tina whispered into his ear, 'You are not permitted to come until I give you permission.'

'Yes, mistress,' he moaned, delighted with her commands. A woman who knew what she wanted from him. Good. Then Tina blindfolded him and tied him more firmly to the bench with his legs spread wide. She pulled out a large dildo and a thigh-harness, strapped them onto her right thigh and then laid her body over Gary's.

'I am going to take your virginity,' she whispered into his ear. 'Make you mine forever.'

'How did you know?' asked Gary, with a catch in his voice. 'Oh thank you,' he moaned as Tina firmly pushed the large latex-covered knob of her dildo into Gary's vulnerable asshole, juiced and closing and opening like a puckered mouth. 'Ahhhh!' he cried in pleasure/pain as Tina slowly buried the length of the tool inside him and then leaned in, firmly keeping it inside him. Gary panted and sweated. Tina looked down at his body, violated lovingly by her, and smiled. She was sopping wet again, she was glad she had forbidden his orgasm. She wanted it all for herself.

After thrusting until she was so aroused she couldn't bear it any longer she slowly and gently pulled out of Gary's body and took off the harness and dildo. She untied him and ordered him to lie on his back on the floor. Eagerly her slave obeyed his instructions, his handsome face serene and gentle as she bestrode him and, slipping a condom onto his erection, which still strained towards her, she firmly slipped his cock into her wet, wet longing and fulfilled it. After she had come several times in quick succession Tina looked down at Gary and said, 'You have my permission to come.' Thrusting quickly into her again he did. Crying out like a peacock in the early morning, marking his territory.

Hoping against hope this will become his territory.

'May I serve you again, mistress?' asked Gary, finally kneeling fully clothed at her feet.

'Contact me when your tour ends,' said Tina, and gave him her business card. Neither of them could make any promises. As they walked out the back of the pub they sagged against each other, satiated, exhausted. Laughing and kissing like teenagers outside a dissolving party.

'Fuck you're good for me,' he exclaimed as she got into her taxi.

Tina grinned. 'I know,' she said as the car drove her away.

Chapter 8

CHEESECAKE

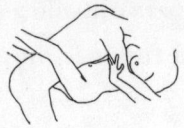

Anne assembled the spring-form pan. Lightly greased it by carefully wiping it around with butter paper. Then put the measured flour, sugar, butter and vanilla into the elderly cake mixer to chug around coalescing into the crust for the cheesecake.

Crust, what a lovely word. Bite deep, sink my teeth into something crunchy, slightly browned, semi-sweet and supportive of my filling. She pressed the dough into the spring-form pan with firm thumb strokes.

What do I want to fill it with? A man of substance, a man of depth. Someone I have to chew to discover his true qualities. Maybe even elusive, hard to get — not like a punch in the face. I'm used to the punch in the face, she thought wryly, it's tempting to look for that again. At least I'm familiar with it. But — someone sweet, creamy, loving and deep like a good baked cheesecake, that's what I really want. She slid the pan into the hot oven.

Not like a stripper, a real bloke is what I want. She felt heat suffuse her body, thinking of those naked men last week. She had come every night since the show thinking about them, their beautiful bums, their smiling faces, their overt sexuality and pride in themselves. Such a turn-on. But – no, she wasn't going to be like Tina and actually go and get one for herself. Too embarrassing, not romantic enough either. Sure you could see everything you were getting but – not the real inner man.

She took the fresh raspberries she had picked free at a local farm and tossed them in a pan with sugar and a little water. Hot and red. Tart but sweet, tangy and tasty. I love raspberries best of all. The pips crunching in my teeth, having to pick them out with a toothpick, the soft texture of the berries, their downy plumpness against my lips and fingertips like the cheek of a child.

Anne felt warm red lips, her dream-lover's lips, enfolding hers in a long deep succulent kiss as she stirred the fruit over the gas flame. She uttered a deep sigh of longing. Blocked her need for kisses: breathed out. Found the yellow cornflour packet in her dark old-fashioned pantry, mixed a tablespoonful with a little cold water and stirred it into the hot sloppy cooked raspberries. The mix thickened immediately into a creamy-thick tangy raspberry topping for the cheesecake. The crust was almost cooked. She put the raspberry sauce aside to cool then took the crisp golden crust out of the oven.

Jamie was sitting watching on his grandmother's knee. 'Me too!' he exclaimed about everything Anne did. Now she let him pour two-thirds of a cup of sugar into the mixer bowl. An ineffable expression of pride suffused his face as he sat back on the bench beside the mixer. He officiously brushed his tiny chubby palms together with the adult gesture of a job well done. 'I help mum,' he said, 'help make 'eese cake.'

Laughing, Anne's mother said, 'Isn't he such a man,' admiringly, then longingly, 'I love your cheesecakes, I can't wait to have some tonight.' They watched closely while Anne opened three shiny, silvery cream cheese packages. Jamie said, 'Me too, me 'uv 'eese cake.'

'I'm glad you wanted one enough to bring me the cream cheese, it isn't cheap and the benefit doesn't give me enough to buy luxuries like this,' said Anne and then she smiled apologetically. 'Actually I'm supposed to be taking the cheesecake to a pot-luck dinner at the school tomorrow night. Do you want to come with us and have some there?'

Her mum frowned and pouted, 'You mean to say I'm a double stooge? Bringing you cream cheese and looking after Jamie while you are cooking for other people and not me and the kids like I expected!'

'Oh mum, don't be silly. You love being with Jamie

and you do alright out of my cooking. Why don't you come to the school tomorrow night and you'll have some fun with both the kids?' She brushed her hair from her forehead; the kitchen was heating up. 'Now what about taking Jamie out to explore the park?'

Jamie slipped down off his grandmother's knee and grabbed her hand. 'Come on, Nanna,' he piped cheerfully, ' 'eesecake la-ter. Car now,' as he led her out the door to her car. It was an easy walk to the park but Jamie loved all vehicles, from tractors and motorbikes, cars and trucks to aeroplanes. Food and machines were his passion and the chance to ride in the car with his grandma to the park and play on the adventure playground was just what he wanted to make his day. If he was really lucky he could get a try at pretend 'driving' the car even though he had to stand on the front seat to reach the steering wheel.

Anne started the clunky old Kenwood mixer. Her grandmother had bought it new and used it for 30 years before passing it on to Anne when she saw that Anne was the cook of the family. The chunks of cream cheese clonked around in the dinted metal bowl before softening under the relentless force of the mixing arm, becoming smooth and creamy combined with the sugar. Anne broke two eggs into the mixture. 'Solid cholesterol, all of it,' she thought as the eggs burst softly and swirled into the creamy filling.

Watching the mixer arm travel around and around, her old fantasy came back to her. The first time she'd had this dream, a waking daydream of love, was when she was ten years old. Something about it still knocked her out, sent her into a romantic trance, gave her fantasies which were just that, dreams that would most likely never come true.

Her prince would come and look deep into her eyes, with his commanding fiery gaze. Her own eyes were grey and boring but his were deep dark fabulous eyes; a lot like those rivers which are peat-brown, full of mysterious gumboot-tea-coloured waters. Rivers which, in rising from underground caves, are full of mystery and a desire for light.

He smells . . . wonderful as he looks into my inner womanhood. Sighing, Anne spooned two tablespoons of flour into the creamy filling, flicked in a pinch of salt and watched as the pollen of the flour became absorbed in the silken body of the cream cheese mix.

He slowly places his arms around me, not carelessly as if he didn't mind one way or the other if he hugged me, but sensuously, purposefully, this is all he wants to do, hold *me*, love me. Then he will softly murmur in my ear, 'Anne, you are the most gorgeous girl in all the world. Please kiss me.' Then I melt, like chocolate in Jamie's palm, hearing his voice, feeling his body pressed close to mine, smelling that man-smell he has. That special odour like vanilla, like crushed rose leaves, or maybe the essence of roast pork or fresh-squeezed lemons.

Skin. The cream cheese filling's like skin, my favourite thing. The kids have wonderful skin, olive like mine with their dad's fair hair. It looks great, I'm proud of such beautiful children. Their skin feels so soft and delicate yet heals up tremendously fast when they hurt themselves. I loved Joe's fair skin. It always felt so exceptionally delightful to me. Kept me going in the times when I wanted to leave him, that lovely skin of his.

But my special lover's skin would feel even more marvellous. Satiny and electric at the same time, tingly like anticipation of a special gift, that moment of desire just before you take the first bite of hot buttery toast after a long walk in the rain. I tingle all over just stroking his forearm.

This dream is so short, so sweet and full of promise. Just those hints of passion, of love and trust, of physical appreciation and — it's gone. Leaving me feeling even more lonely than before. Now I'm an adult I'd like to add bits to it so that when I brush my fingertips over the front of his silk shirt, he gasps. His nipples are sensitive and he presses his whole body passionately to me. He is erect and he leans down, brushes his lips over my nipples in turn. My hands find his rod and greedily I stroke it. He's hard for me, just for me. Drinking in his firmness I glory in the feel of his lusty body against mine.

I flood to the sharp tingling tug of his mouth on my

nipples. Each in turn teased and suckled, wetting me inside and out. Anne swayed against the bench no longer seeing the cheesecake swirling around but seeing instead her fantasy lover made real. Then he —

'Mum!' Sara ran in, her voice piercing in its urgency, shocking Anne from her dream. 'What are you making?' Anne snapped to and turned the mixer off. 'Where's Jamie?'

'Cheesecake for tomorrow's pot-luck dinner at school. Jamie's gone to the park with Nanna.'

'Ohhh, goody, can I go too?'

'Yes, but be very careful crossing that main road now. Look both ways twice!'

'Yesss mum.' She sounded bored with all this fuss and ran out the door. Anne heard her tiny sneakers pattering down the path. She stood at the door and watched until she saw Sara's tiny form run into the park beside the adventure playground. Jamie would be endlessly pretending to drive the old truck cab that was cemented there as a much loved toy for the kids.

Turning back to the mixer she added a cup of cream, vanilla and lemon peel to the filling mix and stirred it gently by hand. Then poured the thick custard onto the cooled base and smoothed it out. She tasted the mix, cool and delicately sweet. Thick and fatty. Delicious, cheesecake, cake of love.

Oh she longed to feel a lovely long fat penis pressing

open her mouth. Her womanhood throbbed as she thrust the cheesecake into the hot oven. Set the timer and began to wash the dishes up. There was no point doing anything else, it was all just too frustrating.

I know which ingredient to put with what to make a perfect cake: melting-in-the-mouth chocolate cake, tart lemon cake. I do a superb baked cod with herbs, smoked fish kedgeree, roast wild pork, plum duff, home-made ice-cream. But I don't know the rhythms, the smells, the caresses which will intimately and ultimately thrill and please me. What will give me the exquisite feelings of my daydream?

Sex and cooking are so close and yet, if you are ignorant of one, so far, so very far apart. Maybe there is a food which will satisfy me so much I won't need a lover, not need sex ever again because that food is so intimate, so sensual, so gratifying that all I would need is more of it.

She finished the dishes and made a cup of coffee. There are lots of foods that are supposed to be aphrodisiacs and there are some, like cornflakes or water crackers, that were designed as anti-sex food too. Weird the things we attribute to food. But it's easier to get food than it is to get love and affection or good sex.

There's a reason for those jokes Tina gave me about chocolate and sex. Ha — chocolate satisfies even when it's gone soft. Any size of chocolate is fulfilling. Begging is unnecessary to get great chocolate. You can *get* chocolate. Which is surely my problem. I can't get any sex, so why not have something lovely like cheesecake to eat?

Good chocolate is easy to find. With chocolate there is no need to fake it – I love it. Mmmmm – and chocolate won't get me pregnant. I can have chocolate any time of the month and noone will get queasy. Strange isn't it? How ironic and simple sex and relationships seem when you compare them to something like eating a favourite food.

I've read about women having a wonderful time in bed. I'm looking forward to the chance to make sex and love into something more resembling what chocolate is supposed to provide.

She heard a car drive up to the door. Tina rushed in.

'Let's go to the pub for a couple of hours – there's a good band playing, we could dance for a bit. I saw your mum down the road, she said you should go.'

'Conspiring against me again, I see,' Anne sighed with mock resignation and then grinned. 'When the cheese-cake's cooked, then I'll go with you. I'll make mum and the kids pasta with pesto and a salad while we are waiting.'

Chapter 9

THE PUB

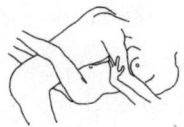

Tina led the way into the pub and moved quickly to the bar. Once there she looked around, focused, exclaimed loudly and hurried over to a handsome Maori man who was leaning his swanndri-clad frame up against the bar.

'Hey Koru! Good to see ya! Anne, I want you to meet Koru. Just out of the bush for a holiday in the big smoke eh?' Tina hugged Koru impulsively. He grinned and said 'Tina isn't it? Howareya girl? Long time no see!'

Standing back from them a little Anne looked at him. His eyes seemed level with her own. He wasn't anything above average height, but his eyes were a startling Scandinavian blue against his dark skin. He had fine dark brows, regal cheekbones, and a long silky-brown muscular neck disappearing into his t-shirt. Deep black hair curled to his shoulders which bulged out under his swanndri, and although Anne didn't look directly she sensed that the rest of his body was as sexy as the top half. She took a deep breath and smiled at him. Just some guy out of the bush, yeah. No worries eh girl?

Then he smiled at her, held out his hand and as her right hand met his she gasped. A kind of electrical shock had cascaded over her from his body. She almost stepped back but was held by Koru's warm firm hand round hers.

'How are ya?' he asked, his eyes looking deep into hers. A dazzling smile following, questioning, as if he really wanted to know something about her.

'Ahhhh . . . fine. Nice to meet you.' Anne found herself breathless, took her hand back and shoved it into the pocket of her jeans.

'Drink?' he kept on looking into her eyes and grinning with those devastating white teeth dazzling her as he took her order. When he handed her a cool glass of beer their fingers met and she shivered again.

Wow! I've never felt a touch like that when meeting someone before, sheesh! What's wrong with me? She sipped her beer and tried to make small talk. After a while she found they were talking about pig dogs.

'Yeah,' Koru was saying, 'my best bitch had two really good pups last year and they are training up well for this year's pig hunting.'

'Got one for sale?' asked a keen-looking bearded guy who had been leaning against the bar near them.

'Nope.' Koru turned to him. 'I don't sell my dogs,

only give them away sometimes. *Only* to people I know are good owners. Having money doesn't mean you are a good dog owner.' He raised one eyebrow and glanced at Tina and Anne.

Anne suddenly wondered what it might be like to own a dog of Koru's, to be regarded by him as a 'good owner'. She blushed a little, wondering what being owned by Koru, being one of his 'bitches', would be like. What would it be like to be valued, loved for yourself, a valuable property, a good bitch? Producer of good pups who would only go to safe loving homes. Yeah . . . somehow she felt that Koru gave love a meaning that went beyond mere association, ownership and sex.

Tina nudged her and whispered 'Ladies', glancing meaningfully in the direction of the toilet door. Anne followed her dutifully, not wanting to be left alone with the blokes at the bar. Tina went into a cubicle and said, 'Whaddaya reckon – eh? I think Koru is a real spunk.' She sighed as she rustled the toilet paper. 'I bet he's not so good as Gary last week but – you can't have everything.'

'Mmmmm,' answered Anne as she reapplied her pale sheer lipstick. Tina might be looking for another bloke tonight but I don't really care, she thought, if I pick up a guy tonight or not. Then a shaft of panic flooded through her. Well – what would I do with a man if I did find one? Mum and Kate are looking after the kids, Tina is paying for the petrol and the drinks. I'm humiliatingly dependent already without getting into trouble with a guy who won't want to take on my kids.

'If he fancied me, I'd have Koru like a shot,' Tina continued, coming out of the cubicle. She rinsed her hands and preened, pulling her t-shirt lower and tighter over her breasts. Tugging her already skintight jeans deeper into the cleft of her ass. 'If he doesn't go for me, how about you — Anne?' She wriggled and grinned happily at her friend.

Anne refused to consider any such thing. To advertise her single state felt shameful. Ladies' night and now this was all too much, somehow. She wasn't used to being on her own with men she didn't know; or going out and being left to drive home on her own either. She felt a tiny bit grumpy about Tina and her man-hunting ways. Her conscience said she should be at home with the kids, not out flirting at the pub.

'Nah, I'm not interested,' she said confidently, using her anger to keep her lower lip strong and then feeling, suddenly, as if she were lying through her teeth.

Tina led the way back to Koru who was still talking pig hunting with the men leaning on the bar. The band was playing loudly in the background so they had to shout to make themselves heard.

'You still going out with Sue, Koru?' asked Tina after listening to a couple of yarns about the bloody fate of several wild pigs.

'Nah — we split ages ago,' said Koru, sounding happy about this outcome. 'I haven't had a girlfriend for about a year now. I'm quite happy about that too, after my experiences with a dating agency. Did I tell you about that?' Koru raised his eyebrows and looked around at Anne, Tina, and the two guys he'd been swapping yarns with.

'Go on, tell us, you're dying to,' urged Tina, grinning. Koru took a swig from his pint of beer and shook his long curly hair until it swung back from his face. He beamed, then winked at Anne and she felt a delicious sense of being included, of belonging here, with Tina and Koru and the blokes at the pub. A feeling she'd never had with Joe and his mates. To them she was just another sheila, a slut, an available cunt. To them anything female was to be taken for granted, exploited, abused, used up like fish bait or a dozen beer.

'About a year ago, after Sue and I quit, I decided to register with one of those dating agencies. I thought it might be a good way to get out and meet women that I wouldn't get to meet at the pub. Well!' he slapped his cheek in gentle punishment for his own stupidity, looked comically up at the smoky ceiling and swigged some more beer. Tina grinned at Anne.

'What a mess that turned out to be! Just about every week I'd drive all the way from Croisilles into town to take a girl out. Buy her dinner and flowers, or take her to the movies and have a coffee afterwards. Each woman was such a disaster I started to think that for sure there was something really crook with me, eh? Or some really dud deal going on at that dating agency.

'I may not be the brightest guy around – my ex would probably say I was all booster, no payload. But boy did I get some dim bimbos shoved onto me to go out with. Maybe it was that I was a nice guy and the woman running the agency was giving me all the 'new' girls to try them out and report back. I dunno.'

'Well – what happened?' asked Anne, interested despite herself.

'Well, she gave me real flakes to call. You know, dizzy girls who want you to explain the movie to them. Who have no idea what the items on the restaurant menu are. Ditzes who giggle at everything and can't have a conversation about anything more interesting than the weather. If you try to talk about politics or religion or Maori culture they just look dim and repeat the last thing they said about the weather or ask,' he mimicked a falsetto voice, "What does that mean?" Then if you tried to explain whatever it was they'd get upset and refuse to talk to you or act like there was a hole in their bag of marbles and ask to go home. As flaky as a snowstorm most of those girls I took out. If I was lucky I got one as bright as a night-light.

'I wonder, you know, if it's some electricity in my hair that attracted all these flakes to me?' He grabbed a lock of his hair and shook the dandruff out of it, looking at it in mock surprise. 'Do I look like the kind of guy who always gets the girls who are several beers short of a six-pack?' Koru sounded so simply bewildered yet full of humour about it that they all laughed. Tina reached up and stroked his abundant black locks.

'Nah,' she said, 'I don't feel anything out of the ordinary.'

'Thanks, babe. There was a woman who was *worse* than the flakes. I had this one who really did the nasty on me. We had talked on the phone and agreed to go out so I duly turned up at her flat with a bunch of flowers for her and I stood around waiting for her to be ready. There were four women there, friends or flatmates, sitting in the living room with the TV blaring. I chatted about this and that, you know how it is when you are waiting for someone.

'Finally the woman I was waiting for came out, just dressed in jeans and a t-shirt and she said to all the women there, "What do you think of him — girls?" and all the girls just put their fingers down their throats and made vomiting noises at me. I was really shocked at their behaviour, you know. I would never have treated one of them so bloody rudely and after that I told the agency to stick their service up their ass. Not before dumping that stupid bitch in it though. I hope the agency kicked her off the list, nasty little cow.'

'Makes you wonder what these people who put their names down with agencies are looking for doesn't it?' Anne shook her head, feeling glad she hadn't answered any ads. She was becoming aware that if Koru had turned up with flowers for her she might have had a very different reaction.

'Well *I* think you're gorgeous anyway, Koru. I just don't get to see you very often. Are you in town much these days?' Tina leaned back against the bar and thrust her breasts out.

'Yeah — I'm going for a part in a show at the Operatic Society next week and I'm working part-time, whatever I can get to make ends meet. Hunting and bone carving are all very well but I can't make and sell enough pendants to make a living.'

'What do you carve?' asked Anne, looking at him and wondering how he would get a part in an opera. He didn't look the type. Koru reached inside his shirt and pulled out a large complex taniwha design in flecked whalebone. It was truly impressive. Anne and Tina touched it reverently. As she stood close to Koru, Anne became aware of how his body moved, of a vibrant electricity which flowed from him to her, of the smell of him, warm and doggy, familiar like her own bathwater. She surreptitiously sniffed in his odour as her fingers travelled the veins and ridges of the carving, warm from his skin.

'My whanau have a good stash of whalebone and I am

always being visited by the local taniwha so I carve him in lots of different ways, as well as making other traditional designs, manaia birds, fish, sometimes tiki.'

'Wow — that's gorgeous,' Anne breathed, looking at Koru with a deeper appreciation of his talents.

Tina drank down her beer and ordered another one. 'Hey,' she said, nudging Koru, who was looking at Anne as Anne looked at the taniwha pendant. 'Weren't you on stage at ladies' night the other day?'

'What? Oh, yeah. I had to stand in for one of the guys who had to go off early. His wife was having a baby at the time. You shouldn't mention things like that, Tina. I wasn't supposed to be recognised.' Koru sounded only mildly peeved. Anne looked at Tina. 'You didn't tell me that you knew any of the strippers,' she said in amazement.

'Well I wasn't *sure*,' Tina said. 'Until just now when Koru told me that he was definitely up there. I thought I heard his voice when I was with Gary but then,' she paused dramatically — 'I was *busy*.' Koru giggled a high laugh full of humour and Anne smiled into his eyes. He looked at Tina and nudged her.

'I heard about that. You *are* an inventive girl, aren't you? Quite had Gary hooked. And you know how many women a week *he* runs through.' There was awe in his voice and Anne wondered what Tina had done to get this reputation from just one encounter with a stripper. Then she decided she'd rather not know, thanks.

'Which one was Koru?' whispered Anne to Tina, who was smirking smugly remembering Gary on his knees as she gazed over Koru's shoulder into the flashing lights strobing the dance floor. After a moment Tina shook herself and pulled Anne close.

'He was Zorro, the one with the black mask and red cape, surely you remember him? He's got a fabulous body, even though he doesn't work out like the other guys. He only strutted his stuff once, more's the pity.'

'Oh.' Anne wasn't sure now if she could remember Zorro. There had been so many different acts with the men dressed differently, acting separate roles each time they came on stage and all of them so incredibly sexy. She mostly remembered her own arousal, painful after months of nothing. Her body waking up as if a switch had been flicked inside her, opening up to the possibility of pleasure.

'Do you remember which one was me?' Koru asked, looking into Anne's eyes. She blushed and dropped her eyes unconsciously to his groin, then realising where she was looking she stepped back and said, 'Um . . . no. There were so many of you and I was just enjoying all of it . . . really . . .' she ended lamely. He struck an attitude, hips thrust out in Spanish dancer pose, twirled an imaginary cape and spun around ending in a crouch looking up at Anne, grinning like an Olympic winner. He looked sexier than any man she could remember, his hair tumbling around his shoulders in a profusion of delicious curls. She took a deep swallow of her beer and almost choked.

'Zorro — the terror of Croisilles harbour,' Tina teased him. 'You are always showing off to the girls and never landing any.'

Zorro stood up, shrugged his shoulders. 'Yeah — well. I've just never met the right girl yet, that's all. I will one day, don't you worry about that. I have wonderful qualities that you know nothing about, Tina. Sure, I'm a bit jealous of Gary, lucky bugger. But those strippers get all the pussy they can cope with. More, actually. I'm not into that sort of thing.'

'Don't you believe him, Anne. He's a slut like all those strippers. Three-women-a-night men. Screwing till they can't keep it up.'

Koru looked shocked, placed his hand on his heart and said jokingly, 'Who me?' then he relaxed the act, looked at Anne and said more soberly, 'Gary may be able to hack that kind of pace but I've been invited to do a circuit of the country with them and turned them down. I don't get turned on by just *any* woman that wants me for her own lustful needs.' Tina moved over to him and slung her arms around his neck. She grinned up at his face and pressed her body against him. 'Not even me, Koru?' He gently disengaged her arms and stepped away.

'Not even you, with all your delightful charms,' he said

firmly. For some reason Anne felt relieved by this exchange. There was no reason for her to doubt Koru's word about his attitude to women. He seemed to be in his late 20s, talented, good-looking, yet on the lookout for the right person. Just like she was.

'Come on Tina, leave the poor guy alone. Whatever you did with Gary is enough to impress him. Let's have a dance, we *did* come to have a dance, didn't we?' Anne tugged Tina's arm in the direction of the dance floor. Tina laughed, blew a kiss at Koru and his mates and elbowed her way through the crowd to dance with Anne right up in front of the band as they pounded out old Elvis, Beatles and Neil Diamond numbers.

When they returned to slump, exhausted, at the bar, Koru had gone.

Chapter 10

THE TASTE TEST AT SCHOOL

Anne carried the chilled raspberry-dripping, whipped-cream-decorated cheesecake into the school hall and placed it carefully in a gap amongst the other desserts. Periodically, hungry children would run over to the dessert table and Anne could see their little mouths watering like hungry Labrador puppies over the pavlovas, chocolate cakes, date loaf and fruit salads sitting there in plastic-covered glory.

She blushed a little thinking of the pent-up sexual energy which was cooked into that cheesecake, and stood aside in the window looking at all the parents and children milling around. Meeting and greeting, recognising and chatting, they were mostly strangers to Anne, since Sara had been attending this school for only six months.

She felt heavy, listless. Ready for anything and yet empty of purpose, just waiting. Almost concentrating on stasis, willing nothing to change while desiring something, anything to change so long as it gave her more than she had.

The main course was served and everyone crushed in a cheerful queue to get their meal. Anne filled plates for Jamie and Sara and then for herself. There were lots of salads, baked stuffed potatoes and an excellent huge cheesy lasagne. Jamie sat beside her eating with all the concentration that hunger generated by playing with a dozen other toddlers could bring. She helped wash up the dishes in the kitchen, chatting with the other women who were cleaning up.

When the dessert table was pulled out into the centre of the throng, Anne took a long sharp knife and thrust it deep into the centre of the cheesecake. The knife pierced the deep rich circular kiss of raspberry and whipped cream on the top of the cheesecake and swooped down into the concentrated tangy body of the cake to effortlessly part the crisp vanilla-flavoured base.

Because there were so many people she tried to cut the cake into as many pieces as she could, slim slivers of delicious concentrated rich dessert. As she cut slice after slice she became aware of a presence beside her, the hairs on her left arm prickling with the proximity of another. She glanced up quickly, but just met with a black t-shirt before she had to look back to cut the next slice. Then the person standing there said with a slight snort, 'Those slices are too small!' Anne looked up again and saw a grinning rosy mouth, slightly crooked teeth and a pair of deep blue eyes looking into hers.

She gasped and a tingle flowed through her. Koru leaned down and she saw that his long curly black hair was tied in a ponytail, which was perhaps why she hadn't recognised him before. He greedily selected not one but three slices of her cheesecake and slid them onto a paper plate, then he picked a sliver up in his fingers and ate it, biting slowly and deliberately, looking intently at Anne. He ran his long moist tongue around his lips. Anne could hardly bear it. She felt like she was hyperventilating. Sara ran up to her and said in her high piercing voice, 'Mum! Mum!' and Anne, relieved from the grip of Koru's eyes, said, 'What darling?'

'Mum, Jamie's getting into the water.'

'Oh my God, not water again,' muttered Anne. 'See you later,' she called over her shoulder and hurried off with Sara to rescue her stroppy son who wanted to be in the fishpond more than anything. When she had carried Jamie well away from the pond and cleaned as much mud off him as she could, she settled the children on a rug in the hall and hurried to get them some dessert. The puddings had disappeared fast and there were only small amounts of the largest ones left. The last mangled piece of cheesecake lay forlornly on the plate and Anne quickly took it for herself. She bit into it, feeling that this cheesecake was somehow special, better than the previous ones she had made; there was more emotion in this cake, more passion, more love.

It melted softly in her hungry mouth. She shut her eyes in enjoyment, ahhh . . . Relaxing, she took another bite and then felt that presence beside her again.

'Gidday,' he said, his voice deep and sweet-sounding. Her eyes sprang open.

'Kapai te kai eh?'

'Hi. Yes it's delicious,' said Anne, trying to be casual.

'Did you make that cake?' he asked.

'Yes, did you like it?' she smiled at him, knowing he did.

'Yeah, there wasn't enough of it. I could have eaten it all on my own,' his voice so deep she shuddered. 'Your kids?' indicating Sara and Jamie playing where she had left them. She nodded. 'Great cake, lovely kids.' Then he reached down, touched the side of her mouth. 'You've got a bit of raspberry there.' He scooped it up with his finger, moved the finger to his lips and, looking deep into her eyes, he sucked the dab of raspberry off his finger.

Anne's stomach turned over. What an intimate gesture he had just made! How dare he do that? 'O God, O God,' ticked over in her head. Here was some kind of delightful male alien with psychokinetic tentacles which were expertly weaving their way deep inside her body. She felt suffused with a pleasure which had never, except in her dreams, been evoked by a man.

Suddenly the scent of his body washed over her, flooding her senses with an overwhelming sense of lustful male energy. Testosterone set off waves of response deep within her. Then she staggered, hit by two hungry children who were missing out on pudding. Koru didn't leave, he began to dig out ice-cream for Jamie while Anne helped Sara to apple pie and cream.

'Didn't we meet the other day at the pub?' Anne asked, slipping a spoonful of fruit salad into Jamie's ice-cream-smeared mouth.

'Yeah. Koru Mahakipawa's the name.' He held out his long brown hand and she shook it, shuddering as the warmth and electricity flooded into her from his body.

'I liked you from the first moment, didn't like your friend Tina, though. She's a bit over the top, isn't she?'

Anne blushed, remembering how shameless Tina had been with Koru that night. 'I thought a bloke like you would go for a sexy hot woman like her,' she said, feeling she had nothing to lose.

'Nah — you know that. I turned her down flat, don't you remember?'

'Yes, I do.' Anne grabbed a handful of serviettes, crouched down and began quickly and efficiently wiping Jamie's face and hands. Being busy stopped Koru seeing that her hands were trembling.

'Do you know why?' he was looking down at her,

grinning. He didn't even move when Jamie grabbed hold of his jeans with a creamy, grubby hand.

'No, why?' asked Anne, not looking at him, trembling inside, not daring to think. Caught in the headlights of his voice, his touch, his eyes and mouth.

'Because I fancied *you*, that's why.' His statement was a straight fact. 'Still do, actually.' He knelt down beside her, gently reached out and turned her head to face him.

Shyly, as she had never felt before, Anne raised her lashes and looked up at Koru.

'Would you go out with me on the weekend?' he asked. 'Whatever you want or can manage. Movie, coffee, dinner, tea at your mum's, anything so long's you'll see me again.'

'Yes,' Anne whispered, feeling shy and overwhelmed. Jamie shoved up against her and she sat down suddenly on the scuffed wooden floor. Koru stood up grinning widely and held out his hand to help her up.

'At my feet already eh?' he joked.

Chapter 11

WOMAN HUNT

It was hell getting away from home the first night Anne went out with Koru. The only one available to look after the kids was Tina and she insisted on bringing around her latest catch. A ditzy blonde bloke who tittered whenever Anne said anything to him and hung continually off Tina, draping himself around her shoulders like a fox fur.

Anne shuddered as she walked away from the noisy chaos inside the house. Koru had been waiting outside the gate for twenty minutes already because Jamie had to have his nappy changed and wouldn't let anyone but Anne do it. Then he had thrown a tantrum for ten minutes at the thought of Anne going out without him and not reading him a bedtime story. He had finally fallen asleep, still sobbing and Anne tiptoed down the path hoping that if he awoke it wouldn't be until she and Koru were well down the road.

She climbed onto the bench seat of his ute next to Koru and he grinned at her. 'No,' he said, 'Don't apologise, don't say anything. I didn't mind waiting. I have lots of cousins, nieces and nephews the same age as your kids and I know what it's like, trying to get away.' Anne rubbed her face tiredly, then she giggled. Koru started up the ute and began the drive into town.

'What's the joke?' he asked. Anne laughed louder until she almost couldn't stop.

'I told Tina that you met me at the school do and chatted me up. She was really envious, even though she's got herself a new bloke tonight.'

'Was she now?' Koru laughed, his handsome face crinkling up and hiding his blue eyes. 'She does nothing for me. I don't want a woman who is just going to lead me on, tempt me, torment me, suck me dry and dump me for some other poor bugger. Tina seems to be that sort but you don't.'

'No,' said Anne, 'I suppose I'm not.' She told him the sordid history of her marriage to Joe. 'We've been apart a year now and I'm slowly getting used to having a peaceful life with no one hitting me or manipulating me. It's heaven, really.'

'I bet it is. The guy sounds like he's got a coupla kangaroos loose in the top paddock. No one in their right mind would hit a lovely woman like you,' said Koru driving fast but not so fast he scared Anne. 'I'm taking you to a special little café I know of, it's out of town a bit but I like it. I noticed you are into food, and *this* café has special food.' Her heart beat faster. He had noticed she was into food — how did he figure that out?

It was the first time she had eaten ostrich meat and it was delicious, served with a salad of wild green leaves and summer fruits with sweet new potatoes. A local olive grove provided the oil to drizzle over it all. Anne savoured every bite. Koru impressed her again and again. He had reserved a special private table and after they had eaten dinner but before dessert, a huge bunch of flowers in glorious reds and yellows was delivered especially for her. He presented them to her with an old-fashioned grace and eloquence which melted Anne. She'd never had a man give her flowers before. They smelled wonderful.

Koru pointed out that there were three red roses in the bunch. 'They are to represent love, passion and lust.' He looked into her eyes and touched her hands as they clasped the bunch of flowers. Anne blushed and the blush travelled from her face to her neck and down to her breasts and then lower, warming the small of her back, her thighs and lastly she tingled deep inside. The blush deepened so much that she ducked her head, burying her face in the fragrant softnesses of the multicoloured petals. A pulsing began that started as a low vibration welling outwards through her whole body. Koru was gazing at her, smiling and waiting.

'Thank you,' said Anne almost inaudibly to the flowers. 'Thank you.'

Koru leaned forward and whispered, 'I love you!'

She shuddered, gasped and cried out, 'Oh! Koru! How can you love me when you hardly know me?' He caught one of her hands in his.

'Look at me, Anne,' he requested softly. Trembling, she gazed at his handsome features. What can he possibly see in me, she wondered, and is he just too good to be true? 'I want to be your man. Your friend, your lover, if you'll have me. If I'm the right kind of guy for you,' Koru said firmly.

Anne smelled the flowers and thought about him. She looked hard at Koru and said, 'You aren't one of those Maori guys who hits their women, are you?'

Now it was time for Koru to blush. He shook his head, his whole body vehemently anchored to her hand. His hand gripped hers tightly in reassurance and then relaxed. 'Because I've *had* abuse from my man, had it up to here,' she gestured at the crown of her head. 'Now I'm looking for love, for good sex, for someone who will really *care* about me and my kids, not just themselves. I haven't had much experience with men, Koru, I don't really know *what* I really want or need. But those things are a must.'

'I'll see you right, girl. I'll do my best. I'm sorry about the blokes who beat their women. I dunno what gets into them, unless they are acting out their hate of their mothers, some psycho-shit like that, maybe. Yeah — and I know us Maori are pretty bad. But I've never hit anyone, never wanted to either. If I feel like a bit of violence I just go out and do a bit of pig hunting or fishing.' He sounded real and sincere. Anne felt she could give him the benefit of the doubt. She smiled at him.

'Ok, I'll give it a trial run. You and me, friends first, and if you look like you remind me of the ex too much, well I'm off. I won't tolerate violence in my life any more.'

Koru looked delighted, his smile blindingly happy. 'You and me?' his hand was sending her electric signals again. She sighed deeply in relief, her tension eased. Now she could relax, look into those incredible eyes and say honestly, 'Yep — I'll give us a go. What have I got to lose?' Life was suddenly more interesting with Koru in it. With this gorgeous Maori hunk wanting her, interested in knowing her. A delightful extra was the delicious frisson of knowing that he preferred her over Tina. That was a turn-up for the books. Boy was Tina going to be pissed off at the news!

❦

'When can I see you again?' Koru asked as he dropped her off after a delicious chocolate and chilli dessert.

'I dunno, it's really hard to get babysitters with the kids being the age they are. Mum likes to have them sometimes but I've used her up for this month. Usually I go round there and cook for her and the kids and then I can go out for a couple of hours. Joe is supposed to have them for the weekend but — I won't know till Friday if he's got the weekend off work or not.'

'Well,' said Koru, unfazed by all this complexity, 'I'll be in town again tomorrow night: Sunday. What about dinner again then, after my rehearsal?'

'What rehearsal?' asked Anne, surprised.

'Oh yeah,' Koru grinned bewitchingly, 'I'm starring in a musical the Operatic Society is putting on — *The Rocky Horror Picture Show*. He got out of the ute and struck a pose. 'I'm just a sweet transvestite — from Transylvaniaaaaaaa!' he sang loudly.

Anne laughed, delighted. 'I've only seen the movie once,' she exclaimed, 'I loved it!'

'Well,' Koru thrust out his chest proudly, 'I am the hero Dr Frank-n-Furter — a scientist with a difference.'

'Wow! Really!' Anne exclaimed.

'I had to sleep with the director to get the part but — you do what you have to do to get a part like this,' said Koru in a breathy falsetto voice, then he stage-whispered, 'NOT!'

'Oh!' exclaimed Anne, laughing, 'I really don't know whether to believe you or not. You are a real tease!'

He walked around the ute to Anne's door and opened it. She stepped out and he immediately caught her to him. She pressed her lips to his and her body seemed to dissolve into his. Then his hard, fit body seemed made of supplejack and he twined around her like eels. She realised as his first kiss moved on to a second and third meeting of their lips that her body was trembling with incandescent desire. It was a strange new feeling for her and she liked it. They stood for a few moments, looking at each other. Breathing fast. Enjoying the pleasure of arousal.

'Oh – I really want to see you again,' said Anne, 'even if it's just to get a few more kisses like those.'

'Ya not bad at it yourself, for an amateur,' grinned Koru. 'Let's get to know each other better – what about coming pig hunting with me out in the Sounds weekend after next? I'm off back into the bush tomorrow after the rehearsal.'

'Um – let's do coffee after the rehearsal tomorrow night. Then I'll try to arrange with Joe to have the kids so I can come out and meet your whanau. Maybe stay at your place and possibly do a bit of hunting, if the weather is OK.' Anne was thinking rapidly. Her life was changing in moments from one of boring solo-motherhood to one where she had a friend, a male to be with, someone else to include and make arrangements for. Oh help!

'Right-oh. See you tomorrow then,' said Koru cheerfully. He kissed her gently yet passionately goodbye, got into the ute and roared off down the road. As Anne walked up the path to the cottage she could hear both her children crying hysterically. She sighed.

Chapter 12

PIG HUNT

It was always going to be difficult but Anne at last twisted her sister Kate's arm and persuaded her with a bribe of chocolate cakes made for her every week for a month to look after Sara and Jamie while she visited Koru at his bach for the weekend. Kate looked at her doubtfully.

'He's a *Maori*?' she repeated. 'Are you sure he's OK?'

Anne was exasperated with her family's attitude towards Koru. 'Joe was white and look how he treated me! Koru can't be any worse, can he? Not without actually killing me.' She chucked her backpack into the back of her barely registered car.

'I'm just going out to spend a weekend pig hunting with a friend. That's all. Don't make a big deal out of it. OK?' She kissed and hugged the kids, told them to behave for Auntie Kate and drove off. It was an hour and a half of continuous driving to get to Koru's place. He had drawn her a map which she had no difficulty following but her car made heavy weather of the rough track that led to a narrow path through the bush. By the time she thought the exhaust would fall off or the sump bottom out if the track got any rougher, she at last saw Koru's ute parked up ahead at a steep angle on a low rocky outcrop.

Her heart beat fast. She felt nervous but free hoisting her backpack onto her shoulders. Anne had been thinking about her outrageous friend all week. She still couldn't say she loved him, though he said he loved her. She wanted to find out more about him before allowing her heart to commit to a relationship.

When she thought about sex a chill fear gripped her. She stopped on a level part of the narrow track, panting, and looked out at the harbour. Calm and still it reflected the bush; out beyond the heads the surf crashed in from the Tasman Sea. It was a peaceful yet dramatic scene. She could hear dogs barking up ahead. His bach couldn't be far away now. She shuddered, trying to shake off her worries that she wouldn't be good enough for him, that her body was too old and child-worn, that she wouldn't know how to make love with him.

Koru was sitting in the sun, three dogs lying at his feet, when she walked into the clearing. The dogs immediately jumped up, barking in loud confusion, and ran to her. Laughing, Koru called them back but ignoring him they raced around her, tails waving like flags, sniffing and licking all of her that they could reach. Anne grinned at Koru, unfazed by the dogs. He had warned her to expect them.

Koru ran towards her and enfolded her in a bear-hug so warm she melted into his arms. Lifting her face to his, he tenderly ran the tip of his nose over hers and she smelled him, the intimacy of his personal space, his world out here in the bush with the ocean and she felt welcomed, at one with it all and home. His mouth found hers and closing her eyes, immersed in the delight of his mouth gently loving hers; Anne felt a presence beyond them and their pleasure, a green-eyed creature enjoying their passion, their connection. Was it the taniwha? Out there just beyond sight?

'Nau mai, haeremai. Welcome to my whare. Wanta cuppa?' asked her friend when their kisses had come to a temporary end. The dogs had slumped in the sun or the shade, bored with her now. Koru disappeared inside the bach and she looked at his home. It was a curious sight, originally a plain two-roomed box, with a gabled roof rusting from the salt spray. A lean-to housed the kitchen and bathroom; the toilet was a long-drop set apart from the house but connected by a trellised walkway. Everything was delicately festooned with pieces of driftwood hung from nylon fishing line, giving the effect of a mobile house with movable boundaries when the wind blew.

Inside it was sunny and cosy. Fibreglass buoys and pieces of shipwreck and wrack decorated the fireplace and a fire flickered in the coal range. The kettle was beginning to whistle as Anne walked in the door, dodging the mobiles made of shells and nylon fishing line hanging on either side of the opening. Circlets of pig tusks formed a pattern on the wall over the small table and a big pile of paperwork cascaded over the flat surfaces of an old colonial kitchen dresser. A heavy stained curtain hung across the kitchen, dividing a third of its area off. It was pulled back revealing Koru's carving workshop. Several polished guns, none of them new, were stacked in a rack near the door. Koru had two mugs and a plate of biscuits set out on the table and he poured the hot water into the teapot.

'That's right, have a good look around,' he said heartily. His eyes never left her face as she opened the door and went into the small living room which had a natural stone fireplace and was gloomily lined with worn books of all ages. A huge and comfy-looking old sofa was drawn up in front of the fireplace where a neat stack of cut driftwood was stacked. Two Tilley lamps hung from the roof and there were matches, candles and a candlestick on the table beside the sofa.

Anne blushed as she went into Koru's bedroom and found it surprisingly tidy. She sat on the bed and looked around. The small sash window gave a superb view of the harbour. A large wardrobe, two battered chests of drawers painted cream and green and a tiki print taken from the *Te Maori* exhibition calendar finished off the décor.

Koru sat down on the bed beside Anne and put his arm around her. 'This place was where my grandparents brought up five kids. The kids slept in the kitchen behind the curtain where I work now.' Anne smiled at him. Her body felt good next to his, warm and cosy and yet exciting. 'I've got free lifetime use of the place and if I want to move into town one of the cousins will come out and look after it for me. I do have to pay the rates and keep it in good nick though. My nieces and nephews are next in line.'

Later they went for a walk down the track to the beach. The bush was thick, regenerating after farming had failed to make a success of the poor ground. The beach was glorious. Anne lay sunning herself on the sand among the pipis, cockles and driftwood, listening to the bellbirds chiming a delicious treble overlaying the roar of the waves out beyond the harbour bar. She began to relax.

The dogs ran and barked, chasing each other madly in the sea until they were exhausted and flopped down in the shade. Tip, Bill and Dog were their names. Tip was the bitch and her dugs hung down, obviously having fed many pups.

'Yeah — old Tip — eh? My best pig dog bitch ever.' Koru proudly patted her salty head. 'She's helped me catch many a pig over the years. You're my favourite girl — aren't you?' He gazed into Tip's golden eyes and she looked adoringly back. Anne felt a little left out. I want him to feel like that about me, she thought keenly.

As they were walking back up the steep track the dogs suddenly began barking and ran down into the bushclad valley. Soon there was a crashing noise and the dogs' barking became hysterical in intensity.

'Bloody hell — the dogs have flushed a pig,' shouted Koru and he began to sprint up the track to the bach. Anne didn't know what to do. She hovered on the track uncertainly, ran uphill until she was breathless and then Koru, carrying a loaded rifle, ran past her back down the track and into the bush. She tried to follow him, heading for the source of the barking, but he was too fit and fast for her. She stumbled and slid down the steep hillside, bush lawyer and supplejack catching at her, trees looming up to block her path.

She came upon the group of dogs just as Koru did. He had misjudged the creek bottom and had to run uphill in the knee-deep water to find the deep cave-like spot where the dogs had bailed up the pig.

The pig was a huge shaggy black boar with sharp white tusks. As Anne watched, Koru pushed the bolt of the rifle forward to load it. He yelled at the dogs to call them off so he could take a shot at the pig. Bill and Dog came to his side but Tip suddenly rushed in, leaping for the boar's ear with her snapping teeth.

'Giddout of it ya bloody stupid dog!' yelled Koru but it was too late. The boar tossed his head and ripped Tip's belly open with his tusk. Her body was flung aside into the creek and the boar charged, straight at Anne.

She had never anticipated that pig hunting meant that suddenly she'd have a huge wild boar with razor-sharp tusks dripping blood charging at her.

'Don't move!' shouted Koru and then a shot rang out. The boar staggered and turned aside, just missing Anne's body as it plunged into the creek beside her and sank to its knees squealing and grunting, threshing in the water as it died. Koru plunged into the bloodied creek water, swiftly drew his hunting knife from the belt sheath he always carried and cut the pig's throat. More blood swirled into the clear clean water and washed down over the body of Tip.

Koru swore softly, left the pig and sloshed down the stream to his precious dog. She had landed in the shallows and, miraculously, was still alive. Her entrails were exposed by the long slash in her belly. Koru, with tears in his eyes, lifted Tip carefully out of the water, carried her upstream of the pig and washed her wounds tenderly. 'Silly old bitch,' he muttered to her. 'Silly old bitch. What'd ya do that for eh?' The dog whimpered and shivered.

'Will she be alright?' asked Anne, trembling.

'Maybe,' said Koru, standing up with a grunt as he lifted the dog out of the water. 'I've seen dogs survive worse than this, it's a clean cut and I'll sew her up when we get back up to the whare. Bring the gun up will ya?' Anne looked around, shuddering at the bloodied carcass of the pig and saw the gun lying against a huge tree root. 'It's alright – I made it safe to carry.' She picked it up and they began the slog up the almost vertical valley, zigzagging to ease the grade and give themselves a footing in the dense undergrowth. Tip was silent. Koru held her pressed tightly to his t-shirt, now soaked in blood. Anne panted behind him carrying the gun which appeared to be made of lead, it was so heavy. Dog and Bill panted behind them.

When they got to the whare Koru said, 'Get us some clean newspapers from in that cupboard there. Yep – now lay them out in a thick layer down there in front of the range.' He put Tip down on the newspaper in front of the fire then washed his hands in antiseptic solution and cleaned the dog's wounds again. Then he dug out a first-aid kit which seemed to have everything in it that a bush hospital could need stowed in a red fishing-tackle box. He hunted for the right things then threaded up a suture needle with some thick thread.

Anne watched, alternately fascinated and horrified, her body trembling constantly with the shock of the past few minutes. 'Now, Anne, I need your help.' Koru's voice brooked no alternative. She sat beside him. 'Now move around behind her and hold the wound together like this — yep — OK, I'm gonna sew the old girl up, aren't I Tip?' The dog opened her eyes and whined a little then she sighed and relaxed on the newspapers.

Koru's long deft fingers began the task of sewing and soon he had the huge gash securely closed with firm stitches, the flesh meeting cleanly. Tip's shaggy brown fur was held out of the way by Anne. She had closed her eyes for most of the job but the vision of that wicked razor-sharp tusk effortlessly slicing Tip open; then her belly falling apart like a ripped bag of balloons, kept rerunning horribly in her brain as if she had a dodgy DVD jumping back and back over the scene in her mind.

As soon as the job was done she went outside and took some deep breaths of fresh air, then she vomited at the foot of a flax bush. Trembling, she went back inside.

'Cuppa?' Koru offered. She nodded. 'I didn't exactly intend that we should have so much excitement when we went hunting.' He put the kettle in the centre of the range hotplate. 'My neighbour told me he nearly bailed that big bastard of a boar up on his place a few nights ago but he got away. Must have holed up over here thinking he was a bit safer since my dogs are usually tied up. Are you alright? You're looking very pale.'

'I'm OK, just a bit shaken by everything. Do you think Tip will be alright?'

'Yeah — well I hope so. Too early to tell just yet. I must say you stayed calm down there, for a novice hunter you were damned good.'

'Was I?' Anne was surprised. 'I didn't do anything. I should have run away or something but I just couldn't move.'

'Made it easier for me, I could shoot the bugger and know I wouldn't hit you. If you'd run I would have had a hell of a job to kill that old boar and not you.

'Ya know what?' asked Koru, stripping off his bloodied t-shirt and jeans in the bathroom.

What?' asked Anne, sipping her tea and beginning to feel a little better.

'We gotta go down and gut that pig and hump the carcass up here before the other pigs get to him and eat 'im.'

Anne sighed. She felt tired already.

'You pig hunters enjoy this — do you?'

'Yep — it's more exciting than mouldering away down at the pub.' Koru walked into his bedroom in his underpants. Anne felt warm that he was able to relax like this with her. But then she remembered he was a stripper and she didn't feel so special after all.

Chapter 13

DON'T DREAM IT, BE IT

Anne sighed in contentment as she lay in a hot bath, steaming in the dusk-filled bush behind the bach. Koru had lit a fire under the bush bath after they had finished toting the pig carcass up the hill. It was an exhausting and bloody job but the haunches, shoulders and head of the pig now hung in the meat safe which was a cave dug into the hillside behind the bach. It had an ingenious mesh door that kept animals and insects out. Stars twinkled and the sickle moon was just setting on the edge of the horizon. Far below her the sea glittered faintly in the starlight and the sound of quiet lapping water suffused the air.

Koru walked over to the bath, naked. Anne ran her eyes over his superb body: his long slim legs, muscular chest, the gold rings piercing his nipples, his sensual full lips and bright eyes, his lovely hair and hands. Part of her swooned every time she was with him. Just looking at him was a feast for the eyes. She felt somehow dowdy and unworthy of his attention.

'Ready to share yet?' Koru asked, his white teeth showing up in a grin.

'Oh — yes. Get in.' She had never shared a bath with anyone other than her kids. Koru got into the bath and began to massage her feet, slowly and gently. She began to relax even more, the hot water and his deft fingers easing all hurt and tightness from her body.

'How's Tip?' she asked.

'Not bad now, eh?' said Koru beginning to soap his body all over. 'She sat up and had a drink before. Always a good sign. She thinks she's in heaven being allowed to lie there by the fire. She's never allowed inside when she hasn't got pups.' Koru stood up and soaped his legs and genitals vigorously. Anne watched, fascinated by him. Her body had begun to ache with wanting and yet Koru hadn't made any real advances towards her.

Were they going to sleep together tonight or would she use her sleeping bag on the sofa or lie on the floor beside Tip? Well she'd find out. She knew what she would prefer. Koru rinsed his body off and Anne realised that he was displaying himself for her and she grinned. Shyness was morphing into desire, fear transforming into lust. Koru had saved her from the charging boar. How could she thank him enough?

Koru got out and wrapped a towel around his waist. 'Had enough?' he asked. Anne nodded and stood up, a little shaky on the timbers that lined the bottom of the bath. Koru steadied her, wrapped her in a big soft towel and insisted on carrying her over into the house. He took her to his bedroom and placed her softly on the bed. She lay there feeling safe and warm. After lighting a couple of candles Koru began to trace her face with his fingers. She sighed as he explored her body slowly and intimately. She unwound the towel from his body and stroked his chest, moving determinedly down to his erect penis.

The texture of his sex – the smell of him – was just right. Anne's body leapt into life, awakening like Sleeping Beauty from her cobweb-covered bed. As Koru began to suck on her nipples she wound her legs around his, writhing as the sensations his body was giving her awakened her inner body even more. He began to grip her, feel her with his beautiful strong hands, grabbing her bottom, her back, her breasts in a frenzy of delight in her body, her skin. 'Oh Anne,' he breathed, 'you are as beautiful as I imagined.'

This man is my dream come true, she thought as he pulled her on top of him and she laughed, sliding over his silken skin, feeling her arousal dripping between her thighs, knowing that this night would be one she would treasure forever and, best of all, that there was no hurry, no hurry at all. She had been afraid that bad old memories would block her enjoyment of sex but delighted herself by just being there with her lover and not thinking about anyone or anything but him.

Koru pulled her to the edge of the bed, knelt on the floor and pressed her thighs wide apart. He began to touch her labia with gentle fingerstrokes, moving closer and closer to her clit. She gasped and sighed, the sensations were incredible. Her body had never felt touch like this, never!

Then before she knew what was happening a different touch began and Anne looked down to see Koru blissfully licking her, whispering to her as he licked, 'I love you, sweet wet woman. I want to lick you until you are pouring, pouring into my mouth and then I am going to fuck you, slide into you on your hot wet juices. You are a gorgeous wet woman. Delicious tasting woman. Beautiful woman.' Tears came to her eyes. She had always felt as if her cunt were a bit dirty, horrible perhaps. Joe had never even looked at her genitals, he had just thrust into her without appreciation, without touching. Now she was learning the joy of being relished for herself. Her tears flowed as Koru varied his tongue strokes from tiny flicks on her clit to thrusts into her vagina and then firm long flat strokes up and down her inner lips until she cried out, flying off the bungee platform and plunging, convulsing in ecstasy, precipitated into the wilds of an orgasm such as she had never experienced before.

As the feelings subsided another searing delight raised her body to further heights. Koru stood and rubbed his erect, dripping penis all over her open begging sex. He slipped a condom on and slowly slid into her, arousing exquisite sensations of completion and fulfilment.

Anne gasped, cried out, 'Oh yes!' pulled him deeper into her and as Koru began to slowly thrust she wept again, feeling a joy, a pleasure astronomically beyond what she'd ever been able to imagine connected to sex, climbing Everests of physical delight together, step by step, thrust by thrust, Anne's body coming again and again until finally, with a deep cry, Koru buried himself within her and she felt the pulsing of his semen as it pumped into the condom against her cervix.

It was as if ultimate bliss had burned them to ashes. They collapsed onto the bed and oblivious to the lumpy damp towels beneath them, they slept wrapped around each other.

Chapter 14

TANIWHA

'Is it . . . is it always that wonderful? Making love?' Anne asked in wonder, ashamed of her ignorance.

Koru grinned at her as he made them a midnight cuppa. 'I dunno,' he said honestly, 'but I think it's our responsibility to find out, eh?'

'More practice?' suggested Anne, grinning too.

'Oh – definitely, *lots* more practice.' Koru placed her brimming cup and saucer in front of her and sat down to sip his. 'Ahhh, I needed that,' he said a few moments later.

Anne added two spoons of sugar to her tea, stirred it and drank it down.

'I'm ready for more practice,' she said and stood behind Koru, burying her lips and nose in his hair, smelling the sea and a hint of pig and blood and dog on him. From the rug Tip looked at them through half-open eyes, the stitches a garish reminder of the day but her gently wagging tail evidence that she was mending.

Later Anne said, 'Oh! I just can't get close enough to you, not as close as I want. I wish I was an octopus. Then I'd have one arm caress your face and mouth, one suckered to each of your nipples, two snuggled around your lovely long legs, one holding your gorgeous tight bum and two smothering your cock and balls.' She shuddered in delight, thinking of holding him so intimately. 'Just think of all those suckers caressing you!'

Koru opened his eyes and looked into hers. He smiled dreamily and said, 'Well I'd have to reply to that by becoming my taniwha self. My three-fingered arms and legs would enfold you, penetrating you in every orifice. The mouths of all my manaia attached to your clit, nipples and mouth. My skin wrapping around you, my scales rippling against your skin. Loving the feel of you. The taste of you. My jaws cradling your lovely head. Then I'd slowly enter you with my huge green phallus. Your body, open, wet and fertile as the ocean would wrap around me and we'd flow together like a river in flood pouring into the sea at the Rakaia. We'd be a snaking green deluge inundating all the braided shoals.'

Anne shuddered and wound her fingers deeper into Koru's hair. Then she slid her hands down his neck and shoulders until her arms wrapped around his lithe silken body. She stroked up and down the beautiful slabbed

140

muscles of his back and chest, her palms drinking him in as his big hands cupped her buttocks, his thigh pressed against her mons. Her legs twined around his as best the long rigid bones could manage, not being octopus tentacles. Their lips met in a long soft breath of a kiss and before she knew it Koru had fallen asleep, his mouth still on hers, his breath coming soft through his lips and his limbs relaxing their grip on her body.

Anne lay there, awed by their loving, feeling his body, experiencing his physical love for her since his body remained glued to hers. She visualised his taniwha self making love to her. A supernormal entity, a dragon-like beast. A creature of myth and of a unique energy that belongs to this land. Alien yet one with her. She could almost feel his scales against her skin. Outside a gust of wind roared through the trees and hit the bach with a crash. The dogs woke and began to bark crazily outside.

She opened herself to him and he entered her like a firestorm takes a forest. Their bodies writhed in ecstasy for a few timeless incandescent moments and then the feeling was gone. Koru lay, still sleeping, in her arms. Anne glowed as an ember of coal, late at night, will give out its essential heat. The wind rushed around the bach and roared away into the night. The dogs were silent once more and she slept, breathing the breath of her lover and knowing a peace of body for the first time.

Chapter 15

BLOOMING

Tina looked Anne up and down. 'Well—what a difference! For the first time in your life you've been well fucked. What a change!'

Anne blushed. 'What do you mean, a difference?'

'Well, just look at you.' Tina propelled Anne to the mirror. 'Your hair glows, your skin is blooming, your eyes are alight, you are walking on air. Wow! I'm jealous . . . well nearly.' Tina stopped.

'Why only almost jealous?' Anne asked, laughing at Tina. Everything made her laugh now. It was Tina's turn to be embarrassed.

'Gary turned up again last night. He wants to marry me.'

'What? That's amazing! You really *did* something to him, didn't you. No—don't tell me. I don't want to know the gory details. So—what are you going to do?'

'I don't know.' Tina looked a little trapped. 'I haven't been asked to marry someone for years and years. I haven't even thought about the possibility. I'm too old to get married. But — it would be kind of nice to have just the one partner. The crowning glory is I can't fault Gary on his sexual technique.' She wriggled deliciously and smiled a dreamy smile.

Anne grinned. 'Well give us plenty of notice, will you? It will be hard to adjust to you having the same guy month after month and not having to remember new names all the time. Did you get rid of the last one — the drippy one who hung off you all the time?'

'Oh — yeah! What a wally *he* was. If he had a brain cell it would have been lonely. Decorative but dim. Fucking him was like having a ghost in the bed, all the appearance and none of the substance. I won't have to put up with that kind of shit if I stick with Gary. He will do anything I want and he's well qualified as a physiotherapist, he doesn't have to do strip shows all the time. That is just extra cash he uses to restore old motorbikes.'

'Do it,' advised Anne. 'Don't think about it, just do it, girl.'

Chapter 16

OYSTER, OYSTER . . .

'I wanted you to see photos of my past so you can get to know me better,' said Anne the next time she met Koru for the weekend in his whare, as he called his home. It had been two weeks since they had had the chance to spend another night together. She found it harder and harder to cope without his smile, his body.

'I'll show you mine then,' Koru said, 'after you've shown me yours.' He laughed wickedly and tickled her. 'Mind you, there's a lot to be said for not knowing people. It's a hell of a lot easier to get on with people you don't know.'

'Is it?' she asked, lying back and looking up at him.

'Yeah.' He leaned over her, gazing at her lovely long hair, her loving eyes and hoping, hoping for her true deep love, her understanding. 'When you don't really know someone you can always live in hope. Hope that they will be who you want them to be, need them to be for you. When you really know someone, often you can see that what you hoped for just isn't there; more than that, it is *never* going to be there for you. Then you've only got one choice.'

Anne ran her hands lovingly through his hair. 'What?'

'Leave,' he said simply.

She could see the sadness on his face. 'This has happened to you before, hasn't it?'

He sighed. 'Yep. I'm willing to start over again, though. With you.'

'I'm willing to take the risk — with you too.' Anne felt equally hopeful and fearful of what their relationship might bring to her. She pulled his head down and kissed him with a long, lingering, reassuring caress. They both sighed and turned to the pages of her tatty ageing photograph album.

Yellowing plastic cover sheets which held and protected the photographs were now falling away from the sticky striped white backing which was also yellow around the edges. Fluff and dust had ingrained itself under the plastic, the result of Sara not being able to simply look at the photographs, she had to take them out and play with them too. Photo corners had come loose from their mounts on the black paper pages. Some corners had ripped out and the perforations around the ring-binding in the centre were worn and tatty with age and use. Jamie had scribbled over some pages with his crayons. Life had struck history a blow in the pages of her album.

'See, here's me in the new entrants at school. God I hated that old bag. She taught me nothing but misery.' Anne pointed to the mild-looking teacher who blobbed to one side of the rows of tiny children perched uncomfortably on wooden seats.

'Is that you?' Koru pointed uncertainly to a skinny girl with blonde-streaked bangs which hung untidily over her face. There was a wide gap between her baby teeth.

'Yeah, that's me, although how you guessed I don't know. I don't think it looks like me.'

Koru grinned at her and giggled. 'Yes it does! It does to me.'

'Now — that was Marie, my best friend. I lost track of her after Sara was born.' She sighed. 'It's really hard to keep track of old girlfriends when they change their names all the time.

'I remember trying out kissing with her when we were about ten. We really wanted to kiss boys but we were too scared to do that so we kissed each other instead. It was embarrassing but lovely.' She skipped a few pages of various relatives and family reunions. 'Now there's the first and only guy I'd ever had — until you.' She smiled at Koru. Her finger rested on a small blurred shot of a spotty blonde youth with a scowl on his face. 'Joe,' she explained.

'I took that photo when we had been going out for only

146

a week. I thought I was happy then – but that was nothing to what I feel with you now, Koru.' She leaned over and kissed him softly. The softness evolved from buttery strokes to melting candyfloss. From the crumbling sweetness of a melting moment to the drowning gasp of the swimmer as she goes under into the depths of inner space.

Several minutes later Anne found herself wound around and over Koru, both of them flushed and panting, hearts beating fast. He looked into her eyes and giggled. 'I love you girl,' he said huskily; then, morphing into Frank-n-furter, asked wickedly, thrusting against her with his hips – 'Isn't it *nice*?' Pressing his erection against her mons. Anne swooned into his passion, adding hers like petrol whooming up the flame into a micronuclear incident.

Slowly she undressed him, rediscovering his glossy silken skin. Just touching him sent shivers through her.

He lay beneath her, allowing her to strip him of his t-shirt and his jeans, his grey marl G-string bulging with the force of his erection. A damp patch growing there as she stroked her full breasts over his chest. Then she sank down and began sucking firmly on his nipples, the gold rings piercing them clicking gently against her teeth. Koru began to moan in ecstasy, slowly thrusting his hips up and down between her legs, breathing fast, his eyes shut as he enjoyed the feelings of surrender and desire flooding through him.

Anne stood up and stripped off her shorts and panties. Already wet with desire for him she lowered herself down between his legs and pulled off his G-string revealing his rampant erection dripping, begging for her body to join with him, her own body aching for his to be within her. She decided to put off the moment of union by licking and sucking him. She began to pump the skin on his penis, slowly slid the silken foreskin down over his knob revealing the slick juicy apex to his sex. She gently began to lick him, forcing more moans and sighs from his mouth, slack and open with intense delight.

The taste and smell of his sex flowed through her, confirming her desire for him, ringing up a firm transaction on the cash register of her body-mind. No doubts, no thoughts of anything but the moment, the penis in hand. Sucking him, humming over the end of his glans, Anne had Koru convulsed and ecstatic. He stopped her before he reached the point of no return.

'Come here, girl,' he said, changing places — his voice Mae West: gravelly and seductive. Anne relaxed and lay back as Koru spread her wide, admired her body. 'Man, oh man . . . I love your body, you are so gorgeous,' sliding down until his mouth hungrily buried itself in her mons.

Anne lay shuddering as he tongued her expertly. Now she was getting closer to seeing herself through Koru's eyes. His comments about muff-diving and how much he loved sucking her sex ran through her mind.

'I love licking pussy,' he said, as they sat on the rocks fishing for cod. 'What *is* it about having a lick?' he wondered to himself. 'I think it's the texture, all those little valleys, the sweet silky grooves of the vulva. Then there's her thighs tightening around your head, the little quivers of delight and tension. The thrusts of her hips into your mouth and all the time I'm diving for seafood, trying to suck that little oyster off his mound.' His tongue was in the best spot, the most *sensitive* spot . . . ooohhh! How did he do that? Anne gasped and sobbed, surrendering to his mouth.

'Oyster, oyster you are making me so keen. Oyster, oyster, you are making me take a deep breath to go down, deep down between,' Koru sang as he raised his head, deliberately teasing her. He grinned as she gasped and pumped her hips, deprived of his touch, and lowered his dark head between her thighs once more.

'My talented arero, my Maori snake-tongue slithering up and down between her clefts all wet and slippery. Oh — it's beautifully soft almost slithery on the bottom and rough, almost raspy on the top. I like the contrast, the taste, the smell of an aroused woman.

'Mr Arero darts around the little clit making her stand up so proud, begging for more. That little mound begins to thrust, push and push and then her long delicate hands come down and pull you in and if she can't reach behind your head she'll grab you by the ears! I bent down to kiss her sweet lips good night, she closed her thighs and broke my glasses!'

Anne laughed, relaxed, trusting him. Her crotch wet, sloppy and comfortable with joy, with lust. Delighting in his mouth, his keen and loving tongue and lips serving her pleasure.

His tongue like a steel whisked through her, sharpening her senses, honing her body with pleasure. Anne spun out and out into the universe until she felt that her whole body filled infinity with a fine web of rapture spun fine yet strong and thin, straw spun into gold. Her body a Rumpelstiltskin, hiding her true name, the reality of her pleasures until now, this month, this year, this heaven.

Crying out, calling her thanks, she came, cascading back into her body in shuddering increments as Koru held his mouth warm over her clit, being there, present and loving as she passed her orgasm to him in waves of delight which made his erection harder and more eager to work for both of them.

'One thing that's always the same . . .' he'd said, 'is the intensity of a woman's orgasm. It's exactly the same with all women. Mind-blowing power if she's been sucked off properly. When a woman comes it's like marinated fish; a little like lemon juice and fish juice; or liquorice and lemon juice. The orgasm comes out very sweet to the tongue which is tired, stretched and swollen, in need of some sweetness. A woman's juices make your tongue swell up.' He didn't get a chance to say any more about muff-diving because the cod struck the bait all at once.

Anne's fishing line jumped taut and she dragged in a big struggling blue cod while Koru hauled on his rod and reeled in two smaller cod at once.

Chapter 17

PHOTOGRAPHS

Koru rummaged through the pile of photos he had pulled out of a shoe box from under his bed. Anne lay on the bed dozing after her orgasm.

'Oh, yeah! take a look at this one!' he exclaimed and giggled wickedly. 'I'd nearly forgotten about this woman.' Anne looked at the photograph. It was of two gorgeous women in their early twenties. She raised her eyebrows at him. He pressed his finger over the prettiest one.

'See her? I was at this long boring conference and she came up to me out the back of the marae and whispered to me "I want to fuck you." So I arranged to meet her outside the grounds in a park I knew of. I went there, not really expecting her to turn up at all but she did! When I began feeling her up she was so eager, so wet and horny, I just leaned her up against a big oak tree, parted those long lovely legs and fucked her, right there and then.' He grinned at Anne. 'I had her coming all over the place. Who knows who heard us? We both had partners at the conference but they didn't seem to miss us.

'She told me later that she hadn't expected me to fuck her quite like we had, not as soon as I had but I said, "Well darling, you were so wet and hot for me that I just had to go ahead." "You know" — she said, "I was glad you did."' He finished his story crowing proudly, taking pleasure in a job well done, the rampant male advertising his sexuality as if it were a favourite motorcycle he'd just driven into the room with a flourish, ear-splitting exhaust roaring.

Anne laughed and then frowned. 'You're a cocky bugger about fucking women, aren't you, Koru?'

'Yeah, I love women.' He was all simple honesty as he sat down beside her and gently pressed his warm soft lips against hers. 'But that was ages ago. I haven't had a woman I deeply loved in my life for so long I'd just about forgotten what love feels like — until I met you, darling.' She dissolved under his passionate kisses as his mouth moved over her neck and shoulders sending delicious tingles all through her, an excitement which spread again to her mons and deep within her body. She shuddered and sighed in bliss.

'Oh Koru, Koru . . . more please . . . more . . .' but he stopped, began leafing through the photographs again. 'You've gotta know *all* about me before we go any further in this relationship,' he said firmly.

153

'Now here's a photo of me in my evening dress, years ago. Mum took the picture but she was so scared the neighbours would see me she pulled the curtains.'

Anne peered at the faded colour snapshot. 'You dress in women's clothes?' she asked in amazement.

'Yeah,' said Koru matter-of-factly. 'I love it. It feels really sexy and gives me a hard-on without fail.' Anne was silent, still staring at the woman in the photograph. Was that Koru's long glossy curly hair or a wig? Were those really his lips under that bright lipstick? The long golden frock seemed to cover small breasts and a womanly body, it couldn't possibly be him — could it?

'What do you think — eh? Look pretty good, don't I?' Anne felt a chill of doubt, of anxiety, of unreality.

'One time my mum and my aunties didn't even recognise me.' Koru looked at her, wondering about her silence. He giggled nervously.

'Really? You fooled your mum?' Anne was awed. No wonder she couldn't recognise him in the photo! If he really *was* able to fool his mother dressed as a woman, he could fool anyone, even her.

'D'ya want to see me dress up like a woman?' Koru asked eagerly, getting off the bed and standing up, stretching, moving over to his wardrobe. Anne was silent, wondering finally what she had let herself in for. A bloke like Koru, pig hunter, talented carver, actor and singer, stripper and a — a cross-dresser? A transvestite in real

154

life? She had no idea if she could handle this, really take it on board, or even believe it.

'Yeah. Show me, darling. It really doesn't look like you in this photo, you know that, don't you?'

Koru giggled. 'That's the point – eh? Being able to look like someone else, the opposite sex, your girlfriend, is the coolest thing. I love it. If you like how I look then you and I could go out and have a girls' night out on the town together, would you like that?' He reached up to the top of his wardrobe and pulled down a large suitcase.

'Hell, I don't know,' Anne frowned. 'You've just sprung this on me. I love being with you but – a bloke who dresses as a woman, maybe looks more sexy and feminine than I do? That's pretty hard for a girl to take, you know.'

'I really hope you can take it, darling. I love you, but I can't and won't give up cross-dressing for anyone. So I can tell you now that if you really can't handle me dressing in women's clothes then we will have to split. This is something that I've been doing since I was about six years old and I can't quit even if I wanted to.

'My aunties used to let me hang around while they were getting dressed and I'd try on their pantihose and knickers and bras. They thought it was really funny watching me stumble around in their gear. They didn't know I loved the feel and smell of the clothes, the perfume and those lovely women all dressing together. God – the number of times I've wished I was a woman . . .' he ended wistfully, rummaging around deep in the wardrobe.

He didn't find what he was looking for so plonked the suitcase on the bed and snapped it open. There, laid out neatly, were layers of satin and lace lingerie, stockings and bras, slips and knickers of all kinds and colours. There was a cosmetic case and when Anne opened it she found it was full of lipsticks and eyeliner, expensive perfumes and a foundation that matched Koru's bronzed skin.

'You really *are* into this, aren't you?' she said, after smelling all the perfumes and spraying one she liked on her wrists. Then she thought, 'Frank-n-Furter . . . a *sweet* transvestite?' stretched out on the bed and smiled, a tentative kind of delight flooding through her.

Koru searched in his suitcase. He eventually drew out a set of filmy black lingerie: a camisole, lace G-string, garter belt trimmed with satin ribbon and matching stockings. He laid them carefully on the bed. She watched as he stripped and began dressing. Expertly rolling the black seamed stockings up his shapely slim legs. She suddenly realised that there were no hairs growing on Koru's legs. Was he naturally hairless or did he — shave? She had not noticed his hairlessness before.

Koru snapped the garter belt around his hips and fastened the stockings to it with the garter clips. Then he selected a black satin corset for his waist and asked her to fasten him into it. It was so tight Anne nearly couldn't manage the hooks but after a struggle she had it hooked up, pulling his flat masculine waist into a feminine curve, emphasising his buttocks.

He saw her looking at him and pirouetted in front of her, grinning. She drank in his body, how he seemed to be changing from a man into a woman. Even the shape of his face was somehow different.

Koru pulled on the black lace panties, transparent at the front. He tucked his cock and balls in and twirled again for her. Anne gasped, thinking, 'Who is he? Wow, he looks great! I would never in a million years have imagined him wearing clothes like this but now he is . . . it seems to suit him. And it is *so* sexy!' She grinned at Koru and gestured for him to continue dressing.

Koru was looking in the wardrobe and brought out a long dark fabric strip which transformed into a full-length crushed velvet evening dress when he shrugged it on. It just covered his nipples and nipple-rings, framing his elegant collarbones, and the shape lightened the weight of his shoulders somehow. The frock split up almost to the hip on the left side, revealing the black stocking top.

Anne sat on the bed, silently watching this woman emerge from her male lover before her amazed eyes. She licked her lips, enjoying the visual feast, thinking, 'I'm glad he's doing this of his own free will, I would never have dared to ask him to dress as a woman for me in a million years!'

Koru hauled a bundle of shoes out of the bottom of the wardrobe and hunted among them until with a crow of delight he held up a spidery bundle of black straps and stiletto heels which transformed on his long feet into elegant strappy evening sandals of black velvet trimmed with gold embroidery.

He preened and turned before her. 'Whaddaya think – eh? I'm just a sweet transvestite . . .' His smile was radiant and lascivious as he thrust his hips towards her.

Chapter 18

TAHUNANUI BEACH

Anne was deeply wearied by the need to slather sunscreen all over Sara and Jamie but it had to be done or else they'd suffer sunburnt misery for days. The children had inherited their dad's blonde good looks and probably her crooked teeth. She shoved Jamie's sunhat further down on his small head.

Jamie crouched flat-footed and patted the sparkling surface of the sand, then dug into it with his chubby fingers and carried the sand to his lips. Anne watched, shuddering, as he rubbed the sand into his mouth; then she giggled at his grimaces as he spat the grit out in grey dribbles down his chin. I suppose the only reason we adults don't eat sand is that we all tried it as toddlers and learned it had no food value. She looked down the beach for Sara.

Sara was jumping in the shallow transparent wavelets

as they slowly advanced up the shore with the incoming tide. She looked like a ballerina with her long brown legs under her bright yellow bathing suit with its tiny blue-trimmed skirt.

'Gidday,' said a male voice behind her. Anne's spine tingled as she felt Koru's presence. For a moment she tilted her head back, looked for an instant into the sun and felt her heart leap into life as if the bliss of being with her kids on the beach wasn't enough. Suddenly life was more complete. The ultraviolet and infrared of the sun blazed down hotter on her skin and she quivered with delight and surprise.

She spun around. Koru stood there, a shirtless bronzed god with tumbled Adonis hair.

'Thought I'd find you here,' he said, grinning. His intensity, how he drank her up with his bright eyes and seductive smile, melted Anne and she blushed under her calico sunhat. Then she hugged him and his lips met hers in a kiss that connected like lightning striking between two mountain crests.

'You OK about yesterday?' he asked as they moved slowly along the huge expanse of sun-washed beach, following Jamie as he happily wandered along clutching shells, sticks and seaweed to his tiny chest. Dogs running out of the water splashed him as they shook their coats dry, the sticks they had fetched gripped firmly in their wet jaws. Sometimes Jamie laughed at the dogs and the day, sometimes grizzled to himself. Anne held Koru's hand and squeezed it. How could she describe what she felt?

The day they had shared yesterday had seemed a pithy eternity of a bliss she hadn't ever imagined before. Like a fleeting landing on another planet, suddenly seeing huge vistas of another world opening up before her. A new and unsuspected universe had become available to her in the shape of her lover.

Koru had gracefully paraded his feminine self for her, clad in the lovely long velvet dress. In an amazing transformation Anne had seen a tall, proud, beautiful woman morph from her man. A sensual woman who required attention, seduction, who lifted her leg and placed it on the bed, showing off her long limbs, her high heels, her nude thighs and the dark mystery of her sex hidden under teasing lace.

Anne reached out slowly and touched the silken leg before her, slid her hands up and up to forever. Met by a tantalising expanse of inner thigh and above that the transparent lace panties crushing, barely constraining his erection. Koru leaned down over her, purring in his throat. He ran his long fingers through Anne's hair. She shuddered, captured by the delicious sensations of seeing a woman's lingerie emphasising her man and his maleness, like a soft-focus frame around a precious object.

For the first time she saw a delicate sensual sexuality

appearing from within Koru. A receptivity that enticed her, tempted her to do something, to make something of this moment. This wasn't simply a dress-up day. No, this was something more essential, more sexual than that.

Standing before her, open, revealed in all his femininity so she could plunge into him. Thrust her being into his body — take advantage as she so often had been taken advantage of. A strength suddenly flowed through Anne, a challenge to be something more than she had ever dreamed of being.

She stood up, firmly pushed Koru back into the centre of the room, his dress falling to the floor and covering him once more. Yes! I want to try the man's part, thought Anne, taking control. I want to seduce this woman, take her for mine in every way possible.

She pressed her lips to his, now soft and yielding to her pressure, and pulled Koru's slim body into hers. Wet and wetter she became as she ran her hands over his body, silken with the slinky velvet. He laid his long arms over her shoulders and stroked the nape of her neck through the deepest most passionate of kisses. Held her like a woman in a classic movie greeting her lover. Anne, the hero in fedora hat and coat, stubbing out his cigarette, moving in on her. Koru yielding to the hero with soft sighs of surrender.

Her lover moaned and gasped as Anne bit his neck and collarbones lightly. Slid her hands to his nipples and squeezed them around the gold rings erotically penetrating their tender flesh. Anne found he responded as men didn't usually respond, their nipples being insensitive. With a gasp, a small cry, 'Yes, please . . . oh I love it . . .' he whispered, trembling and shuddering against her body as she pinched his nipples again. Sensitive in the nipples like a woman, oh . . . yes!

Anne pretended he *was* a woman – edged the neckline of the dress down and sucked on his now erect brown nipples. Teasing the gold rings with her tongue and teeth. Suddenly he sank into her arms. His knees had given way with the strength of the feelings she gave him. Anne staggered to hold him and control his fall onto the bed.

Wow – he feels like I did when I was breast-feeding! Weak-kneed when his nipples are sucked. Grinning with delight she pressed her advantage, kneeling astride his prone body draped over the tumbled bed. Focusing deep and long into his dark intense eyes she continued to stroke and pinch and suck his nipples in turn. He writhed under her.

'Oh, oh,' he sighed in ecstasy. 'You've found one of my secrets.' Anne smiled, enjoying his pleasure. The feeling of his constrained erection pressing into her crotch as she slowly moved herself over him was delightfully tantalising.

Koru undulated beneath her, sighing, his mouth alternately full, tensing then slackening, his lower lip trembling with desire; almost a woman, all but a woman.

Anne stripped the dress from his shoulders in one fluid movement, freed her own bare breasts by shimmying out of her t-shirt, and began to rub her nipples over Koru's erect nubs. She began to feel electric sensations chorus though her in a hot harmony of desire.

Songs of delight sang in her as she took more and more control of Koru's body. Kissing him, hard or soft as she wished. Taking the lead, running her hands all over him, enjoying the alternate silk and rough of the tips of the velvet. Slowly she worked her way down his body, pulling the dress off him as she went. Now she approached his feet which were strapped into those high-heeled sandals as if they belonged there. She looked at his toes, prettier than hers, under the dark sheer stockings. She hated wearing high heels herself. Found them unstable, uncomfortable; silly, somehow. But on Koru they weren't so silly, they suited a part of him just as they didn't suit any of her. Anne ran her hands up and down Koru's long sexy legs and dropped the dress to the floor.

She freed Koru's dripping sex from the lace G-string, sliding it slowly down his long legs, over the high heels. Leaving him with just the corset, garter belt, stockings and sandals. She stood back and looked down at him. His hair flowed tousled from his chignon. He lay relaxed, trusting, softly breathing. He was truly beautiful. His eyes never left hers except to look at her full mouth. She'd never had a man lie there, waiting for her move, for her to do what she wanted, get what she needed.

She leaned over him, pressed his legs wide apart, like a woman. Pressed her hand down firmly on his erection, enjoyed the feel of him pulsing under her fingers, warm and silky. Firm and *hers*.

'Anne, oh Anne, fuck me please,' whispered Koru passionately. Lifting his hips urgently, humping against her fingers. A sly smile curled across her lips. All in good time, she thought and moved her shoulders from side to side, back and forth, experimenting with the masculine solidity which had somehow sheathed her body since Koru had strapped on his high heels. A feeling of being in control, of mastering him – mistressing him? It felt good, whatever it was.

She reached down into her handbag and brought out the lube and condoms she'd bought at the supermarket last week, almost blushing at the checkout but then not caring. After all, she bought her pads and tampons there too. She stripped off her shorts and panties and lay beside her lover.

Koru snuggled into her and his mouth latched onto her nipple making Anne gasp with fresh pleasure. She undulated her hips, wanting him yet making plans for what would happen next. Feeling the feral exhilaration of being a jump ahead of her lover. She rose, grabbed

Koru's arms and pinned them with her own.

'You are my *woman* — aren't you?' she asked, grinning down at him.

'Yes, yes,' he answered, eyes half shut. Moving his slim strong body under her, his penis smearing her belly with the fluid of longing. 'I am your Papatuanuku, you my Rangi. I your Wahine, you my Tane. Ahhhhhh,' he gasped as Anne rolled a lubricated condom over his penis and then allowed his erection to slip within her eager body. They breathed deeply in unison as their bodies began to slowly dance around the pivot created by their joining. Thrusting and withdrawing, over and over. She felt herself slipping away into ecstasy and with the small amount of consciousness left to her beyond the hot delirium of Koru within her she bent her head and bit his nipples hard. He bucked beneath her transformed, who was within whom? She could not tell in the whirling delight of the sensations coursing through her body.

Koru's full sweet lips met hers and they melded entirely for long moments; waves flowing between them in pulses of energy. Realising he was near orgasm Anne withdrew her body from him. He gasped and opened his eyes.

'Oh! Why?' he gasped.

She smiled, lubed her fingers, slid them under his taut balls and found his opening. It was pulsing, almost begging her. She slid a finger inside the heat of him and her lover moaned, 'Oh . . . yes! Ohhhhhh. YES!' As she listened to his gasps and watched his face she lowered her sopping, aching cunt onto his jumping eager cock.

As she continued slowly thrusting it strained her wrist a little — yet feeling him deep within her and herself deep within him was a thrill that overwhelmed her with an intimacy she had longed for and now had discovered at last.

He lay motionless with his cock buried deep within her, experiencing her fingers within him. Then, after long moments of her hand moving gently inside him Koru began to thrust into her. His long fingers fastened to Anne's nipples. She gasped, rhythmed her hips to his thrusts as they grew faster, more and more intense until suddenly a brilliant gold flood filled her body, swirling around and around like soapy water in a basin.

She called out *in extremis* as the energy propelled itself through her mouth, joined by Koru's cries of release into her. Her fingers were crushed within him but she didn't notice. Slowly she freed her fingers, wrapped her legs under his body and fell onto his chest. Breast to breast they slept until the chill of night woke them.

❦

Anne stopped, dug her toes into the sand, looked at Koru. He squinted into the sun and her eyes. She smiled, softly at first and then with a dazzling happiness. Quickly she walked away from him. Jamie played happily in the sand at Koru's feet; chatting to himself in sand-dribbled baby talk. A slight frown crouched on Koru's brow as he watched Anne walk away down the beach, looking for something. Soon she found a sharp stick, leaned down, wrote large and swift, her footprints decorating the words with the prints of toes and heels dancing. Then said, 'See!' gesturing wide with her arms.

He walked over to look and slowly a wide smile spread over Koru's face. Relief showed in every muscle of his body. 'I love you,' he read out loud. He swung his arms around Anne. She looked into his eyes, smiling.

'Do you — do you really?' She could see his eyes brimming with tears of happiness.

'Yes,' she said softly and then hid her face in his warm naked shoulder. Koru blinked rapidly and held her tight.

'You're the first one to love me in a long time. The only one who has ever loved me when I'm cross-dressed,' he whispered huskily in her ear. Then he smiled radiantly, pulled himself together, tossed his long dark curls over his shoulder and holding her by the shoulders, asked, 'Will you be my woman, Anne?'

She blinked away her tears and grinned at him. 'Only if you'll be my *girl* too,' she demanded.

'Yes,' whispered Koru.

'Yes! YES! Yes! Yes!' cried Anne, dancing in his arms until Koru silenced her by pressing a long passionate kiss on her lips.

Jamie toddled up to them muttering, 'Yef . . . yef . . . ffffffttttfffff.' Sara ran up too and danced around them shouting, 'Yes! Yes!' in her high-pitched little voice.

Anne caught the children's hands and Koru their other hands and they danced around in a circle on the firm damp sand, the sun blazing. Knife of Nelson burning through the skin and not at all repelled by the sunscreen slathered on.

'You're my Venus . . . my Venus. I . . . love to be with you . . .' sang Anne as they walked home for lunch.

Chapter 19

A WORK OF FICTION

Koru was away fishing for the week and Sara and Jamie were visiting with their dad for the first weekend in months when the envelope arrived: Registered. So she was alone, luxuriating in the quietude of a Saturday afternoon while she opened the long legal letter, wondering what it contained and why she was getting something like this. She hadn't got a driving fine and left it unpaid, had she? Suddenly a deep chill of nameless fear struck her and made her hands tremble. Guilt without sin, a strong feeling of danger filled her with no more of a threat than a long legal envelope delivered personally to her hands.

Then as she read the contents she cried, screamed, laughed and cried again as the enormity of it struck her. Joe was taking her to the Family Court for custody of the children. Joe: the father who never changed nappies, never got up to them at night. Who hurt the kids when he was trying to be kind, who shouted at them as his preferred method of communication. Joe who bought them ridiculous presents because he didn't realise that human affection and cuddles were what the kids really needed from him, not junk. Joe the abuser who had hit her in front of the kids and Sara was old enough to remember . . .

'I hereby apply for custody of Sara Margaret Mains and Jamie Samuel Mains' – names Anne had given her children but on this piece of paper seeming like the names of strangers as she read them aloud. 'Their mother is an unfit mother and I can offer the children a better, more stable home.' Then he tried to prove that she was a slut, a prostitute and a careless absent mother using 'evidence' from his friends and workmates.

Some of the people whose statements about her were in the document she had never met, had no idea who they were.

Anne shook her head dazedly. How could he *do* this? *Why* would he do this to her? Just when things were sorted out and settling down. He must have had to work hard to scrape up anything against her because, quite literally, she hadn't *done* anything like what she was accused of in this affidavit. Koru wasn't mentioned at all – so Joe didn't even know about him.

She had to sit down, almost fell down on the sofa, her hands trembling uncontrollably. The cottage, her safe haven, felt invaded, dirtied as she read Nigel's testimony that he had seen her gang-banged down the pub three months ago by five or six men and asserted that she had enjoyed it. He had signed this rubbish? Nigel and his wife were Joe's close drinking buddies and she had known them well all the time she had been married to Joe.

Why? Why would Nigel get involved like this when they had stood back from the separation and didn't even take sides? Why?

Hell, Nigel had seen her in the supermarket a day after she and Joe had separated and he'd come up for a friendly chat. Talked away about this and that and even offered her the use of his body, 'In case she was frustrated without a real man to satisfy her.' Anne remembered how embarrassed she had been by this, especially as his wife had been shopping in the next aisle, and she'd said, 'No thanks,' hurriedly and moved away from Nigel. She hadn't seen him since.

Dave, Joe's best mate at work, had stated that Anne was a whore who sold her services over the Internet and had two or three men a night. She laughed bitterly. She couldn't afford a computer, let alone the costs of the Internet! All the time she was supposed to be screwing her ass off she had been living in poverty, bringing up the kids alone, completely celibate.

Then she remembered when Dave had come around to visit late one night a month or so after she had left Joe. His latest girlfriend had kicked him out and so he came and pounded on her door. Staggered in and fell over, he was so drunk. He terrified her by swearing so loudly she was afraid he'd wake up the children and when she got him quietened down he grabbed her and forced hot heavy kisses on her. He ran his big rough hands over her body and, she shuddered remembering, declared he'd always wanted a bit from her and he was going to get it now. She managed to escape from his drunken grasp, grabbed the phone and stood in the hall ready to run out the front door. She shouted that she was going to call the cops if he didn't leave.

He became silent then, glared at her with his pig-like eyes and she felt his malice beating against her body, his frustrated violence and lust directed towards her. 'I'll get you, you bitch! Slut!' He shouted filthy abuse at her as he walked out the door and down the path to his truck which was parked across the end of the drive.

She stood, trembling, holding the phone for a long time after his truck had driven violently away, tyres squealing, screeching and skidding around the corners of the quiet country road. Then she rang Rape Crisis and talked for an hour before she felt calm enough to go to bed after locking the house up as securely as she could. She didn't sleep well for months after his visit.

Perhaps, perhaps, Anne thought, perhaps this is Dave's way of getting back at me? Are all these affidavits like this? Are they all from men whom I've rejected when they propositioned me?

On and on it went, fiction after fiction all aimed at discrediting her. Yes, without a doubt she was reaping the results of a celibate lifestyle. All the affidavits were from mates of Joe's who had offered to 'fill the gap' in her life either before or after she had left him. She guessed the two she didn't know were 'mates' from parties where they had groped her and whispered, 'Come on, let's fuck out the back.' She'd declined their attentions and forgotten them, but they had remembered her and the fact that she had turned them down. God knows what they'd have done to her now if she had fucked them all like they had wanted her to!

The weight of it sank on her shoulders like a huge load of dung. She wept and shook; hot and cold chills racked her body. Then she staggered to the toilet and vomited. Vomited out all the lies and filth that those lying bastards were piling on her. After she flushed the toilet she sat there on the toilet seat listening to the cistern filling and the silence of her lonely cottage began to get to her.

How awfully empty it felt with her beloved kids actually away *with* the man who was piling this crap up on her. How vulnerable she was without the comfort of their small bodies to cuddle and smell. How tragically silent it was without their feet running ceaselessly around the house, their noisy play, tears and laughter.

That load of lies was going to be registered at court as

if it were fact! She wept at the injustice of it.

She walked into Sara's room and picked up her pillow. Sniffed the aroma of Sara's hair and then clutched the pillow to her and rocked, sobbing, aching without her little girl to hold. Trying to comfort herself that her daughter was there, was really real and would come back to her tomorrow night as scheduled.

It was Saturday. None of her family were home at the moment. Tina was out of town and Lynne? She hadn't heard from Lynne for a while, not since her last visit. She supposed she should have told Lynne about her relationship with Koru but she'd been too busy to call her. There were no lawyers to call. The one who had handled her separation wasn't the type of person she would want to show this affidavit to.

Koru . . . oh Koru! She cried again, longing for him, and vainly. He was out fishing. No phone, no cellphone coverage either. She shook her head, over and over — why is it that sometimes disasters hit us and we don't even know how vulnerable we are until tragedy strikes?

It was Koru who had woken her body and kick-started her heart. Koru whom she needed right now. In a couple of hours mum would be home. How to survive the day until then?

Anne paced up and down but the feeling of having her world whipped from under her feet persisted, leaving her shaking and frantic. Eventually she phoned Lifeline and poured out her story in a storm of sobs and fears.

She talked of her feelings of humiliation and the ironical injustice of this affidavit, and she spoke of her shame. Her shame at having made the mistake of marrying someone who would stoop to this kind of dishonest behaviour in order to take her children away from her. The fear overwhelmed her in waves as she realised that her beloved children were in danger of spending their lives with their incompetent father if a judge believed him. Constantly she kept on wondering — why? Why would he do this now, when everything had just been sorted out? Why?

The calm woman counsellor's voice at Lifeline reassured her. 'Have faith in the Family Court. Lies like this are presented all the time to the court and the judge will see through the crap. Just be honest and tell the truth. Get yourself a lawyer and fight for your right to have your kids.' The counsellor told her to go and make a cup of tea and waited while she made it, listened as she sniffed and gulped and blew her nose. Suggested that she call her mother, sisters and friends over to visit as soon as possible and have someone to stay the night. She also had suggestions about what to do if Joe didn't allow Jamie and Sara to return home the next evening. This took some of the deadly chill out of Anne's body, knowing she had remedies available, people to turn to to help.

Then the counsellor asked, 'Have you ever tried to be angry without having angry thoughts? Have you ever been sad without having sad thoughts?'

Anne stopped and thought for a moment . . . 'No?' she said wonderingly, 'I don't think I can be sad or angry without thinking something about it.'

'I agree,' said the counsellor 'It's impossible to have feelings and emotions without the matching thoughts. So when you feel these emotions, remember that it is the way you are *thinking* that is sad or angry or negative, not your actual *life* that is bad. There's lots going for you, girl. Call back and tell me how you get on.'

Slowly Anne calmed down. The long legal sheets of filth lay there still, on her kitchen table, but were becoming less powerful. She couldn't bear to look at them again. Her mum picked them up when she arrived, read for a while then said angrily, 'You've never done all this! It's absolute rubbish!' and threw them down on the table. 'You're better off without that moron in your life, darling.' And she put her arms around Anne and rocked her, just like she had when Anne was a child and had hurt herself. Anne laid her head gratefully on her mother's shoulder and cried in relief.

'Don't worry darling,' her mother said, 'we'll get it all sorted out and make sure he doesn't try this trick on again.'

Kate and Michelle arrived and mum decided to stay the night with Anne. They all sat around wondering why Joe would do this thing – why would a guy who had never shown much interest in his children suddenly want custody of them? His motive had them really puzzled until Michelle said, 'Hey — isn't this the first weekend he's had off for ages?'

'Yes, why?' confirmed Anne. 'He has to work most weekends but he does get some off now and then.'

'That's *his* story though, isn't it? You are just assuming he has this weekend off, aren't you? What if — what if he's lost his job? What then?'

'Hell, I hadn't thought of that,' said Anne, rubbing her knuckles into her eyes.

'Well . . . I think *I* know what's going on, if he's lost his job . . .' said mum slowly. 'He'll want the kids so he can get the benefit and a meal-ticket.'

'Yeah!' exclaimed Kate angrily, 'He won't have to look for a job and because he's never parented the kids he will have no idea what being a solo parent full time on the benefit would be like.'

Anne laughed bitterly. 'So all this degradation of me is just so he can go on the benefit and stay at home drinking piss and looking after the kids? He thinks he'll have it easy?'

'It could be,' said Michelle, 'but don't jump to conclusions just yet.'

'Hello everyone!' Lynne breezed in and they quickly updated her on the situation. 'Well I can help this time, anyhow. I know a lawyer who will help you out on this one,

Anne. She's a gun at family disputes and custody. She's won a lot for women I know and I'm sure she can for you too.'

'But I can't afford a lawyer again, just signing the separation cost me about a month of the benefit. We had to live on rice and spuds for weeks to pay that lot off.'

'There *is* Legal Aid, you know. Nadia will make sure you get that. Don't *worry*, it's going to be alright,' she put her arm around Anne.

He was late but Joe did drop Sara and Jamie off on Sunday night. Anne felt twenty years older as both children ran to her and hugged her. 'Mummy! Mummy!' they chorused. Joe grinned at her cheerfully then leaned his head out of the car window as he drove away and shouted, 'Slut!' Anne gasped and hurried the children inside.

'You heard it?' she asked her mother.

'Yes.' She looked up from her knitting. 'Great language in front of the kids.'

As Anne was putting Sara to bed after her bath, Sara asked, 'Mummy — what's a slut?' Anne didn't know what to say. A bad woman? A sexy woman? A promiscuous man or woman? Someone who likes to fuck? In the end she said, 'It's someone who likes to have sex with lots of other people, darling. It's used as a nasty name for people. I don't want to hear you using it when you talk about other people. OK?'

'Yes mummy.' Sara snuggled down. Anne lay beside her daughter and buried her nose in her child's fragrant hair. So precious, so very precious. 'Oooh – it's good to be home,' said Sara. 'Dad's place is cold and messy. But – we do get McDonald's every day.' Anne shuddered at the thought of her beloved children being fed junk food every day of their lives, then tried to relax and read Sara her favourite bedtime story.

Chapter 20

ADDICTION

Koru read the horrible details terribly slowly, or so it seemed to Anne. She twitched with impatience as he laboriously scanned the application to the court.

'Got it in for you, hasn't he, eh?'

'Yes. I dunno why now, why he didn't try this earlier. Try to take the kids off me when we separated? Why now — just when things were coming right for me too!' she wailed, her face screwed up in pain and bewilderment.

Koru scratched his head. 'Is any of it true?'

'Huh — the only part that is true is the names signed on the bottom. All those guys are mates of Joe's and — if only he knew . . . all the filthy stuff they are accusing me of doing — well!' she laughed hysterically. 'They wanted me to do *that* with *them*. Each one of them ended up *demanding* I sleep with him — just because I'd left Joe. Then, when I wouldn't do what they wanted, I never saw or heard from them again. Until now — this is their revenge on me for saying no.'

Koru shook his head. 'What are you gonna do, girl?'

Anne put her head in her hands. She felt chilled to the bone, deeply terrified, ready to throw up in fact. 'I don't know . . . I really don't know. I'll have to fight it if I can. I *have* to keep the kids with me. Jamie's too little to live full-time without his mum, and Sara . . . well the danger of her being sexually abused by — well if not him, then his mates — is too high . . . and I know what those guys are like . . .' she shuddered.

'Well . . . I can't understand why people want to fight over their kids. Just give them to him if he wants them. Ya know?' Koru raised his eyebrows at her. 'Blokes lose the right to be with their kids all the time these days. Maybe he could be a good father if he was given half a chance.'

'Didn't you *listen* to me? They are too little, too vulnerable to abuse, Koru. I can't do that. I really can't let them go to him, it would hurt them, ruin them and I'd be a bad mother. A non-mother without them.' She began to cry, sobbing like her heart was breaking. Koru put his arm around her.

'My love, my love,' he hummed as he held her close, supporting and loving her. Kissing the top of her head. When she calmed down a bit he said, 'Your mum told me Lynne's going to get you a lawyer?'

'Yes, I hope she's a good one. I need it. Joe's obviously

182

going to be unscrupulous and I'm not a nasty type like he is. I don't want to fight for the right to mother my kids. It's not fair!'

Koru looked at her. 'Maybe Joe doesn't want to have to fight for the right to father his kids either.' He paused. 'Whatever happens, you are always going to be their mum, you know that don't you?'

'Yes, I suppose I am,' she said, thinking hard. 'No one can take that away from me, can they?'

'No,' said Koru grinning. 'So don't panic, girl. Just relax and think about what *you* want.'

Later that night Anne lay in bed beside Koru and stared up at the ceiling. The tongue-and-groove stained by a century of living created dark lines across her vision, emphasised by the moonshine pouring in the window. Her thoughts were dark and tormented. The abuse Joe had subjected her to hadn't stopped. When would his attacks on her *ever* stop? How could she take the initiative, quit being the victim and strike back? Who is the real me?

Am I still the little girl I once was? Independent, in charge of what I did next, playing in the sand in summer, crushing the ice in puddles in winter? I think I've almost lost her. She is subsumed in the act of shame, in the act of being socially acceptable. At the sound of a footstep nearby she slips inside the doors of my inner being and closes them behind her, stands there, silent, waiting to be free to play again. Sometimes she feels she must almost lock those doors against the world, against other people.

The inner me is so tough she can murder without anger. In cool calm determination no one can beat her. Yet she is so utterly vulnerable she may melt if you look at her too long. She is so smart she can beat you at anything. Yet she is so dumb, so naive, so gullible she'll miss the obvious; all the while scanning the invisible wallpaper of your mind. Anne sighed, tossed and turned. Visions of her screaming kids being taken away from her in the back of Joe's battered old station wagon tormented her.

Yet — pain is a kind of ecstasy too. I suppose if everyone experienced physical pain as really unpleasant there would be few women having sex or giving birth. Nobody would be playing sport or competing in the Olympics. Pain is transformed into pleasure daily by millions, probably billions, of people. There's a different set of millions giving pain to their partners, especially to women. A gift of love.

Pain means he has your full attention as you lick the blood off your swollen upper lip. Feel the second chip from your front teeth sharp on your tongue along with the tooth marks where your teeth punctured your tongue. The hot and salt scald as your blood drips off your chin onto the floor. You mop it up with a dirty dishcloth and hold a tea towel against your punished mouth. Hot and deep the pain in your innermost being. But you know you have *his* attention too.

I must have been addicted to the pain Joe used to give me, because I kept going back for more. I was ashamed that my man hit me, hurt me. Shame — it's one of those social pressures that makes you do things when you really know better. Shame forces you to tolerate abuses you'd never dream of enduring in other circumstances. I'm still ashamed that I had to leave him, make our marriage die because I was becoming too hurt, too battered and I didn't want my kids to grow up with violence in their innocent minds. I really don't want Jamie hitting his woman, when he's an adult. I know he's only little now, but it all has an effect, no matter how young they are.

Joe never asked if I wanted, truly desired, the pain he gave me. Those beatings which approximated attention. Would his hugs and kisses have equalled a punch? What would a gentle touch from Joe have meant to me? Would I have even *noticed* softness coming from him? Just to think of him in that context makes me want to laugh. He's such a great bloke for being tough. But — if he lives that long, someday he'll be old and soft and doddery — who will he try to punch out then? The nurses in the nursing home?

Anne giggled and Koru rolled over and sighed in his sleep.

I've learned that cowering and trying to hide, ducking for cover doesn't really help protect me from danger. I only look vulnerable when I do that. So — what *am* I going to do? What?

She got out of bed and stood at the window, looked out at the moonshine beaming down on the paddocks and bush. Just think! What stupid men they are, those mates of Joe's. I said no to *all* of them! That's the only thing those stories have in common. They are accusing me of a sexual sluttishness which actually applies to *them*. They asked me for sex on the side and I said, 'Don't be silly, no thanks.'

I wonder if Joe knows that? I bet he doesn't. Unwittingly he's been made a tool of by his mates in an effort to show me, the slut who turned them down, that I can't escape their abuse.

Anne gazed out at the indigo sky silvered with stars.

Then she breathed . . . 'I know what I'll do! Yes!'

Chapter 21

LETTERS

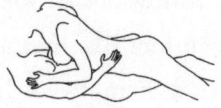

Dear Nanna,

How can I describe it? My whole life has changed. All I can say is my heart is bubbling over with joy because a month ago I met Koru Mahakipawa.

I am in love with him, Nanna. How do I know it's love? Because the happiness I have extends not only to my lips but my eyes, my feet, my heart, my mouth, my fingers. I feel as if I had wings and all winds send me to him — to his arms to nestle safe in his heart.

His whanau are local Maori. They have land in Croisilles Harbour. Koru lives out there in a little bach his grandparents built. He's an exceptional artist, making wonderful bone and jade carvings. Because they are so good, so original, he sells his work almost before it is made. He's a pig hunter and shoots the occasional deer so we have wild pork and venison to eat. I'm busy experimenting with game in my cooking now. I am trying some medieval French recipes combined with local red wines. Oh, you should taste them! If you come up to visit I'll cook a special one just for you. Even the kids will eat venison and pork now.

I know this is romantic babble, but when Koru smiles at me — from the stage where he's acting in a local musical, from the pillow beside me in the morning — I am in bliss. Did you feel like that about granddad?

Joe never smiled at me with love. All he did was scowl. I could do nothing right.

Koru just loves whatever I do. My cooking, the kids — Sara and Jamie love Koru to bits too. I can hardly believe it but they do. I'm hoping to find the time to start computer studies this year and I feel really inspired to cook more than I ever have before. This new year is going to be the best I've ever had. I just know it.

Are you well? I hope so, write soon and tell us how you are. Sara's doing great at school and Jamie, well he's a real boy. What more can I say?

Lots of love
Anne, Sara, & Jamie

Anne sighed as she wrote the address on the envelope and sealed it shut. A happy letter — full of white lies and omissions. There was no point in worrying Nanna about the affidavit from Joe, but omitting any mention of it left a huge gap in the news she could tell, changed the tone of what she could write about. She felt guilty that she couldn't include all of what was really going on for her. To make things worse — today she had received a letter from WINZ demanding that she move closer to Nelson or else she would lose her benefit. She shuddered. The thought of a government department ordering where she could live rankled. Definitely not the land of the free, she thought. I'm in bondage — and I've got to get out.

She was seeing Lynne's lawyer friend Nadia tonight to ask for help with the Family Court and how to write her own affidavit defending Joe's allegations. She was determined to fight to keep the children in her life. The thought of losing access to her darlings because of a bunch of lies concocted by her ex was insupportable.

Legal Aid was all she could look forward to in assisting her to fight Joe if it had to go to court. Anne had been told horror stories about the behaviour of lawyers who accepted the desperately-fighting-but-going-under Legal-Aid cases like hers. People had been driven to suicide by manipulative lawyers when their marriages split up. Some murdered their kids too.

Oh, I hope Nadia isn't like that. Would I be like that? Would I kill my kids to keep them out of Joe's hands? Anne pressed her fingertips into her eyelids. She took a deep breath. No. I don't care how awful he was to me. I really don't believe that their being with him would be that bad. I think Sara has him wrapped around her little finger to judge by the presents she brings home from him. I will have to trust them, and him. Trust that they will be safe. Simply trust. The hardest thing to do.

Anne picked up the letters she had written and dropped them in the post box on the way to get Sara from school.

Chapter 22

KORU

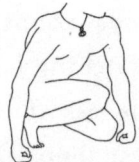

Through the warm day as I weed and fertilise and plant in my garden I watch a mauve and vermilion-pink bearded iris slowly open out. Slowly unfolding to the sun and rain. The thick swollen bud has me thinking of the head of your erect sex, as it unsheathes from your foreskin. Your cock slowly drips clear drops of aroused joy, just like the tips of the iris leaves in the early morning. Dew bedecks the bud tip as the rising sun catches it and transforms it into a radiant coronet of light.

Later in the day the iris unfurls two lobed petals furred with yellow mohawks. I bury my face in the tender tissue of the petals and think of your acorn against my lips.

Ahhh . . . would that you were here and I wasn't looking at flower petals. Instead your bright warm eyes would be looking into mine, your wide dazzling grin, your soft sensuous lips caressing mine in kiss after drunken kiss, your voice huskily whispering, 'I love you woman, I love you. You light my candle, girl.' I descend into your body and you submerge into mine. Our voices calling in soft cries of pleasure, our eyes locked in soul-to-soul embrace. Oh Koru! I want you! Why are you so far, so very far away? I sigh deeply and my breath ruffles the petals of the iris.

Away from you every day seems too long, even though the time is filled with watching Jamie and looking after Sara's needs. The simple task of washing the clothes and hanging them out, letting them dry and getting them in again seems too hard sometimes. I long for your warm arms and legs hugged snug around me.

'Ooohhh come to me, come to me,' Anne sighed, washing the soil from her hands before hanging out the soggy washing.

You're out there in the Sounds. The bright ocean a blue background beyond the branches covering your window. A blinding flash of reflected light when the sun swings around and semaphores incandescence through your window. Bellbirds singing fit to burst your eardrums outside where you feed them honey in water every day, fantails flitting and chirruping because you have no cat to pounce on them.

The dogs panting, waiting for the next exciting outing. Tip healing, lying on her side allowing the sun to heal her belly wound faster. I wish I was her, always close to you, beside you, smelling you, touching you and tasting you. I'd want for nothing, being your pig dog bitch.

Chapter 23

A GOOD LAWYER

'It's not a problem, really. We see this kind of shit all the time.' Nadia was in her forties, blonde hair cut mannishly short with just a hint of spike. Her formal clothes suited her stocky body and she sat oozing competence behind her desk. 'What we'll do is draft an affidavit telling the truth — that you have not done any of the alleged things and that on the contrary you are a conscientious mother who helps out at the school regularly and has lived a blameless life. That sounds like you, doesn't it?'

Anne nodded, relief slowly growing like a bubble in her chest.

'You realise, however, if Joe can prove that he is a good father and parent that he has a good chance of getting the children half the time.'

'Really?' she said, a chill clutching at her heart again.

'Yes, by law the children have the right to equal access

to both their parents and if both can establish that they have a home and can care for the children then the court will see no reason to deny them equal access – especially when you live in the same city.'

'But – what about Sara's school? It's too far for her to go there from Joe's place,' Anne blurted, panicking.

Nadia was calm. 'I'm sure that will get sorted out in time. You told me that your benefit doesn't cover transporting Sara to and from school. How are you managing?'

'Mum and my sisters are helping me out.' She suddenly felt a little silly, insisting that Sara go to a small country school instead of one of the bigger primary schools in town. Yet she wanted Sara to get more attention, more teacher time than she would from a teacher with a big class of rowdy kids.

She knew Joe didn't care if the kids went to a coal-mine so long as they went somewhere during the day. He hadn't shown a flicker of interest when Sara had gone off to school on the first day. Anne had been a mess, crying into Jamie's nappies for a couple of mornings just getting used to Sara being away for five hours during the day. Now, with Jamie going to playcentre three times a week she had one morning to herself and it was bliss. Then a thought stole into her mind . . . If Joe had the kids every other week wouldn't she then have a whole week in which to study or work? Time to herself when she could be with Koru?

'Good for them,' said Nadia in a warm voice, 'but your family can't go on supporting you for years on end, you know.'

'I know.' Anne felt confused and guilty. Maybe she was making a mistake wanting to hold onto the kids with a tight grip. How did she know a city school would be bad for them or that Joe would ill-treat them? When they came back from weekends with him they were happy and bouncy and no more dirty than usual. Maybe, out of her sight, he treated his kids lovingly. Maybe being the child was different from being the wife of an abuser . . . who knew?

'Don't look so sad, Anne,' said Nadia. 'Lynne has invited us out for coffee and drinks at that new brasserie in town in about an hour. Let's work on this affidavit and then pop out to relax and have a good time.' She smiled at Anne and suddenly Anne's head cleared. Nadia was on her side. Someone *was* listening and helping, that was all that mattered.

❧

Lynne sat down opposite Anne and grinned. 'I found out that your sister's guess is correct. Joe lost his job about three weeks ago.'

'What happened?' enquired Anne.

'It's only rumour, but apparently he threatened to beat up his supervisor and that was the end of him.'

'Good job too. He won't learn that violence doesn't solve anything until he's made accountable for his aggression.' Nadia steepled her hands together on the table.

'Most men are violent in some way or other,' she added flatly.

'Koru isn't,' defended Anne.

'He's unique then,' stated Nadia.

'Now where's this Koru?' asked Lynne 'and how come you haven't told me about him until today?' Anne blushed. Nadia and Lynne seemed to be interrogating her — in a friendly way, but still questioning her choice of a man instead of a woman.

'He's away hunting for a couple of weeks, with some mates down the West Coast. He can't help me with the court case anyhow. I don't suppose a Family Court judge would look too kindly on me having a boyfriend who is a pig hunter and acts in *The Rocky Horror Picture Show*.'

'He sounds really interesting,' smiled Lynne, while Nadia looked at Anne steadily. 'More of a goer than Joe, I'd say.'

'Oh yes, he's wonderful, a wonderful lover too.'

'Have you ever made love with a woman?' asked Nadia, leaning forward and clasping her big pale hands together on the table.

'No. I've never really been attracted to women. I suppose if a woman I liked was available then I might think about it . . . but I've got Koru in my life now. I don't need anyone else, not *really*.' Anne suddenly got the strong

197

feeling that Nadia was interested in her. A more than professional interest – she tried to shrug the feeling off.

'I've tried to get her to come out with me to the women's dances but she won't,' complained Lynne to Nadia.

'You should try a woman sometime – you might like it,' said Nadia smoothly, looking deep into Anne's eyes. Then Nadia smiled a sensual smile and Anne blushed as the smile seemed to pour into her deepest crevices. The blush brought a tremble with it as she remembered Koru smiling like that at her.

'I'll get Anne a coffee,' said Lynne, rising to her feet.

'No, allow me,' said Nadia putting out a restraining arm. So her lawyer bought Anne a drink and they began to discuss the situation in detail.

'I suppose . . . looking at it from a practical point of view, I should move in to Nelson.'

'That would be a sensible idea, yes,' confirmed Lynne. 'It won't be possible to live where you are now and not have any income at all. You need to do that computer course you were aiming for, and start working part-time, in my opinion.'

Anne thought for a moment. 'I'd love to start living with Koru but if I did, then I'd lose my benefit, wouldn't I?'

'Yep – most likely,' said Nadia. 'It doesn't make any difference if he isn't earning enough money to keep you and the kids or not. WINZ won't even let you flat with other adults these days, let alone live with them.'

Anne sighed. 'I *have* to get out of this mess. I have got to get a good place to live and somewhere for Koru that isn't too far away either. I haven't asked him if he wants to live with me, or near me, but I can't go and live out at the bach with him. I would have to teach the kids correspondence school most probably and I definitely wouldn't qualify for a benefit living out there. Koru earns plenty of money to keep himself comfortable but it's cheap to live there. There's no power, no phone, no water charges. Just fishing, getting in firewood and fuel for the lamps and heating up the bath.'

'Sounds lovely – if you like that sort of thing,' drawled Nadia.

'But could he – would he come and live in town with you?' asked Lynne.

'Oh – I don't know,' said Anne, irritated with all their questions.

'I have a potential solution to all our problems,' announced Nadia, sipping her beer. 'I've just bought a house – a big old one, right in town here. It's close to schools and probably not far from your ex, Anne.' She sat back and continued, 'The house is in three flats, a big one upstairs and two downstairs. One of them has three small bedrooms. I've taken the top flat for myself and I'm going to rent out the two lower ones soon. So you could have one if you wanted it, what do you think?'

Anne sighed deeply, thinking of her lovely cottage garden going to rack and ruin but she had to face reality — that precious piece of home had to be put behind her and something new taken in hand, for all their sakes.

'Yes, that sounds great. I have to do something, be able to show WINZ I have made an effort towards moving,' she said 'Do you have a key so I can look at the flats?'

'Yes,' said Nadia, 'why don't you come home with me and have a look this evening?'

❧

Nadia unlocked the door and Anne went into the flat ahead of her. The kitchens weren't modern but they were OK. Anne decided that she liked the largest, sunniest flat and to celebrate the deal they went upstairs to Nadia's apartment.

'Do you think Koru would like to move in here too?' asked Nadia, pouring Anne a wine.

'Well, he might. He has to be in town a lot after this hunting trip. He's starring in *The Rocky Horror Picture Show*. It's going to be on in a couple of months, so he has to rehearse a lot to get ready for that.'

'Really? It's one of my favourite shows. What part has he got?'

'Dr Frank-n-Furter. Koru loves the part to bits. He sings and acts superbly and — the costume really suits him.'

'Frank-n-Furter? Is he into wearing corsets and

lingerie?' Nadia looked surprised. Anne thought of his body dressed as a woman and she smiled.

'I think he likes wearing women's clothes more than a lot of women do.'

'He's a cross-dresser then?'

'Yes.'

'Do you like that in a man?'

'Yes — well I have discovered I do, although if I'd just been asked without really experiencing it I would have said no. It's kind of weird, a man dressing in women's sexy things. But I find it really sexy too.' Anne wriggled on the sofa, feeling aroused at the memory of Koru in his stockings, garter belt and corset, ready for his rehearsal.

Nadia sat on the floor and leaned on the sofa close beside her. She sipped her wine and ever so slowly her hand crept onto Anne's thigh. Anne felt the warmth of Nadia's hand and liked it. She was feeling lonely, the kids were with their father for the school holidays and she felt free, unfettered. Maybe life was at a turning point and she could find a new path that wasn't so trapped in solo parenthood. Looking at the flat downstairs made her realise that she *could* live near Koru — if he wanted it. Now she could afford the rent, live in town and still have a big garden to grow food. There was plenty of room for the kids to play outside in the safely fenced garden too.

'I have a lingerie collection, you know,' said Nadia quietly.

Anne smiled at her, surprised. 'Do you? I love lingerie but I can't afford more than the basics right now.'

'My ex-girlfriend was into dressing up. Would you like to see some of the stuff I've got?' Nadia smiled at her warmly.

Anne tingled all over. Suddenly she felt deliciously wicked. Why not? Why not try on some lacy things with the lovely Nadia. Would it hurt her case? *I don't think so*, sang her conscience. Nadia led her into her bedroom and shut the door.

Chapter 24

NADIA

You lie under me and I thrust over you. Watching, listening to your breath gasping in and out. Connecting to the miracle of your lower lip trembling, your upper lip smiling, sighing, surrendering. I vibrate my hand against your crotch. I feel you wet, aroused by me, my body and my kisses. Not a lesbian, eh? I smile gently down as I rhythm myself to your sobs of pleasure.

I evoke soft throbbings within you by using firm undulating thrusts and kisses. My lips and fingers on your nipples. Faster — harder, faster — then slower . . . gently slowing, determinedly withdrawing. Lessening the frequency of your breaths. Slackening the tension to allow your juices to flow more, to persuade your body to like mine more, to give my aching unfit muscles a breather before we both bungee off into the Skipper's Canyon of your orgasm.

You lift your face – press your soft parted lips to mine. You breathe a long breath into my lungs. I breathe back into your body, your breasts flushing, erect over the breath inflating your chest. Rubbing your nipples upon my insanely sensitive breasts you drink me in and thrust against me. Suddenly we are free-falling, tumbling in space, gasping, throbbing, wildly running, rushing towards our orgasms. I hear your hurried breath, your tiny hot moans and gasps in my ear, on my lips. My breaths are as desperate, as vibrant.

Seeking, seeking, reaching out for that golden globe, fingertips trembling with longing. Touching, grabbing at the goal, finally bursting. Our bodies engulfed in glowing plasma we blaze in our privately fuelled sunburst. I hear your cries of delight surround me. 'Oh-oh-ohhhhh!' Rising to a long extended call of ecstasy. You stiffen under me for a few hallowed seconds and finally collapse, imploding. Taking me with you into a long peace without strife or effort.

I raise myself to look down at you. Shudders vibrate your body as you lie totally open to me. Your every hair, pore, sweat gland, ear and throat, grip of thumb and finger, orifice of any kind – open. Open and vibrating to the pleasure I give you.

Mine! You are all mine! Nadia smiled at the thought of yet again stealing a beautiful woman away from a man.

Chapter 25

DISCOVERY

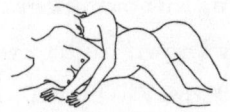

Anne lay beside Nadia. Sated.

She felt completely delicious; her body tingled from head to foot with a glow that she wished would stay but knew would leave her all too soon. Nadia lay curled around her. Anne turned her head slowly. Nadia's dark blonde eyelashes lay curling slightly on her soft cheek.

Her body is as large as Koru's, tall and wide-shouldered with long tapering legs, full of unexpected softnesses. What were firm muscles in Koru were feather-down pillows on Nadia. Her skin delicious, but in a completely different way. Glowing pale, creamy and silken. A soft pink tinged with apricot plus a fine blonde fur swirled over all. A peach, perhaps a large close-up of a rose petal or a honeydew melon.

Turning gently, trying not to wake her too soon, Anne began to explore her lover's body. The belly swelling out softly, her belly-button protruding slightly. Anne had never seen an 'outie' before. She gently moved her mouth over the warm button of sensitive skin. It tingled against her lips with an effervescence she hoped was also evoked in Nadia's skin.

Please let Nadia want me for more than this past blissful week, Anne prayed. I want her so very much I cannot imagine being without her and yet . . . what about Koru . . .? I've only known Nadia a week. Koru a month or so. What about Koru? Why isn't *he* enough for me? Stabs of guilt plunged through her, meteors burning painful blazes into her tender heart.

Anne shifted slowly, restlessly, against Nadia's moist skin and sighed. Wondering about relationships. Suddenly life seemed much more complicated than it had in the awful old days of being married to Joe. I thought that loving Koru and then finding out about his cross-dressing was a challenge but now . . . a woman? Me with a woman? Anne gazed in amazement at Nadia's pubic hair, softly curled and reddish-blonde, creeping up her belly and down her thighs in a soft downy pollen.

Anne's mons was decorated with thick dark curls, a complete contrast to Nadia and she gazed alternately at their bodies comparing, admiring, desiring. Nadia's breasts, pert full latte bowls tipped in peach-caramel, became irresistible once more and Anne began to run her fingers up her lover's body. Sneaking up on those glorious globes resting softly in sleep. From wide thigh over the swell of hip, down to the belly-button, tingles of awareness of the 'other' radiating up from her fingertips as she grew excited again.

Easing both her hands to cup Nadia's breasts. Unhurried and focused Anne stroked and stroked her lover's soft creamy flesh. The supple resting nipples grew firm, extended outward, urging Anne to suck and suck them until she carefully slid down and began to run her tongue around that sweet, firm, crinkled flesh. Erectile but without the potential threat of a penis.

Anne allowed herself to latch on and sucked ecstatically, her eyes shut. Nadia gasped and moaned softly, snugged her hips in closer to Anne. Anne slid her hand down over her lover's belly and — middle finger first — slid her fingers between Nadia's legs.

Unconsciously lifting her hips, Nadia parted her thighs, gasping as Anne sucked deeper and harder on her nipples. Anne's fingers parted those blonde befurred lips and discovered the moist welcoming satin warmth between them as Nadia opened further. Her breath coming faster, her eyelids flickering almost to open although Anne knew that her fingers had not yet brushed the most sensitive tip of Nadia's inner world. Deeper and deeper Anne slid her fingers until Nadia grabbed her hand and pressed her mons hard against

Anne's wrist. Crushing her sensitive bud against the slim solidity of Anne's bones.

Pelvic tilt after tilt, thrust after thrust. Nadia's breath gasping slightly now. Anne felt slippery juices begin to pour over her fingers and, desiring mightily to taste her lover, withdrew her fingers from Nadia and brought them to her mouth. Smelling and tasting the sweet warm oystered musk.

Nadia gasped at the loss, sighed and asked, 'Oh! Why . . .?'

Anne giggled softly. 'Not too fast now,' she whispered and latched onto the other nipple. Her lover now lying spread wide, open like a shag drying its wings, looking for a good warm breeze.

'More, more,' begged Nadia, but she had to wait for Anne to move and Anne was into possessing Nadia's body slowly this time. Anne's thighs were beginning to dampen once more, a fine dew of perspiration sprinkled across her shoulders and breasts. Her nipples hardening, her fingers trembling as she began to explore, alone and without a safety net, no equipment provided other than the human body: The unexplored, known yet mysterious territory of another woman's body. No skills required except a desire to give pleasure.

This was the fifth evening in a week that Anne had spent the night with Nadia; she was shifting into the new flat downstairs during the day. It would be a surprise for the kids when they came home from the holidays. A new home, a new school and a new friend for their mother. All – except the 'friend' – approved by WINZ.

Anne moved to lie on top of Nadia, her softnesses pressing into her lover. The globs in an apricot lava lamp glowing, blending softly, inexorably together. Firmness and decisive pressure from Anne's hips between Nadia's, her pelvic bone crushing in deliberately hard on her lover's mons.

Nadia eagerly lifted her hips, offering her body, her ecstasy to Anne to watch, to enjoy, to delight in her delectable juicy fruit.

Anne sensed Nadia getting close to her ultimate destination and lifted herself away. Knelt between Nadia's thighs, parted her wet labia and gazed at her beauty. The soft glowing folds of her lover's inner pleasure revealed so deliciously that Anne shuffled down and ran her tongue around the swollen bell of Nadia's clit. So deliciously soft and juicy. Like the best kind of sour sweetie in the mouth, a rhubarb dessert, the new pencil eraser you just can't resist smelling and then biting. Biting deeply into its tender, scented, supple resilience.

Yes, Anne wanted very much to bite into that divine softness but stopped herself from indulging in something which would give pain where pleasure was required. Instead she pressed in to grab as much of her lover's tender flesh in her mouth as possible and suck it. Allowing the intensity of her touch to grow from a soft bird-in-the mouth hold to the demanding suckling of a hungry child. From a hungry lick on a melting ice-cream to the gulping mouth of a groper hovering in the kelp.

Nadia gripped her hair, bucked her hips, crying out, 'Yes! Oh! Yes!' babbling, begging Anne to fuck her. 'Please please Anne, fuck me, use the dildo, your hand, anything just do it, lover — do it!' Her cries building in intensity as Anne changed, moved away again. Leaving Nadia bereft, hanging on that vast cliff between desire and fulfilment. Her orgasm trembling, a dewdrop on the brink. Her body arched, demanding just one more touch, one more lick of the tongue, one more thrust.

Anne knelt between Nadia's trembling legs, considered her lover's head tossing against the pillow and decided to try what she longed for. To try to press her wet throbbing clit against Nadia's weeping, begging cunt. She crouched over Nadia, spread herself wide and swiftly pressed her glowing inner lips to her lover's. Nadia almost screamed as Anne, moving with divine intensity, ground her own sensitive nervous system against her lover's. Gyrating slowly she worked their bodies into an orgasmic frenzy of sobs and sighs. Now Anne wasn't teasing or prolonging any more, and soon Nadia froze, her body convulsing internally, gripping Anne's clit in a soft toothless mouth, sucking her into a passionate whirlpool. Anne, feeling the swirl of her lover's orgasm, fell off the cliff of delight and floated down and down into the river of Nadia's femininity. They melted into each other as if they were margarine statues joined at the crotch. Divinely sexed Siamese twins. Slick, juiced, every moment an exquisite pleasure, an unbearable torture of succulent delight. Anne fell down over her lover and kissed and kissed her soft lips, her glowing face, panting and laughing.

Nadia got her breath back and said, 'How did you figure that move out? I thought you hadn't had a woman lover before?'

'I haven't,' confirmed Anne, 'but I've got you to experiment on now so I just thought about it and did it.'

'Here I am,' said Nadia, struggling to kneel over Anne. 'Your organic woman — all for you. If it's going to be as wonderful as this I can handle a *lifetime* of experiments.' She spread her arms, presenting herself to Anne. Anne giggled and ran her hands up Nadia's lovely long pale torso.

Nadia got off the bed and rummaged in a drawer. 'Now take a look at this.' She pulled out a bundle of black straps and a pink and mauve marbled strap-on dildo. She fumbled for a while putting it on while Anne watched, amused.

'Now, I want to try this on you, in you, to see how you like it.'

Anne looked dubious. 'Do I need it?' she asked,

watching the fat firm end of the dildo approaching her vulva. Nadia stroked Anne's clit and swollen lips with the tool. It felt delicious and Anne sighed, relaxed as Nadia began to pleasure her, easing the knob of the dildo into her a few millimetres and then withdrawing.

Anne's body opened, responded, began to beg for more. She hadn't known till now that she ached deep within for some good hard dicking. It had been too long since she had been with Koru and sex without deep penetration didn't satisfy in quite the same way as sex with a penis in use did.

Seeing Anne blissing out on the dildo, Nadia began to thrust it into Anne, deeper and harder, her hips swinging forward, opening Anne up further to her penetration. Anne gasped, moaned, 'Yes, yes.' She saw Koru leaning over her in her imagination, as if it was he moving within her, as Nadia thrust and thrust into her wet, willing body.

'I can tell you are going to win your case.' A wry voice cut across their lovemaking like a samurai sword. Anne gasped. Koru stood in the doorway, his arms folded. A small smile, maybe a grimace of pain on his handsome face.

She struggled to get away from Nadia but her lover wouldn't allow it. Anne saw how it was. Instant competition between her lovers and she was the meat in the sandwich. A deep thrill shuddered through her.

Nadia was too strong for her to fight so she lay still, closed her eyes and mentally left the room. A blush of embarrassment, of shame, bloomed over her body, burning deeper than third degree.

'That's my woman you're fucking there,' said Koru quietly but with a hint of menace in his voice.

'There's no ownership of people in this house,' said Nadia, offended at his attitude as she withdrew her tool from Anne's inner depths.

'No loyalty or faithfulness either, I see.' He moved over and sat on the bed beside Anne's prone body. Nadia lay behind Anne, her dildo pressing against Anne's tailbone.

Koru began stroking Anne's face and moved his long slender fingers to her breasts. She shuddered as he began to squeeze and manipulate them, her body responding despite her shock at Koru arriving back in town early. He stood up and stripped off his jeans and t-shirt, revealing his glorious body, the gold nipple rings gleaming in the candlelight. Anne opened her eyes and gazed at him, at the sleek darkness of him contrasting so divinely with Nadia's fairness, the warm light gilding all of them with a glow, velvet at sunset, vanilla ice-cream melting on glass. She sighed and held out her arms to him.

He lay down in front of her and began to softly kiss her lips. Nadia shuddered but didn't move until Koru had finished kissing Anne's mouth and had moved down her body to her nipples, making her moan and squirm and then to her muff where he opened her up wide, revealing the slick juices aroused by Nadia which he swiftly licked away and replaced with his tongue. Anne — caught — could do nothing but surrender. She humped her hips and arched back against the bed. Nadia took off the harness holding the dildo and dropped it over the side of the bed. Then she took advantage of Koru being between Anne's thighs to position her ample blonde bush over Anne's face.

Anne eagerly began to stroke those delicate pink labia with her long pointed tongue, quickly — gently, back and forth, in just the way she knew would drive Nadia wild.

Koru for his part knew the keenness of the razor of his tongue on Anne's clit and kept up a rhythm that began to have her moaning in unison with Nadia's soft cries of delight. He grunted and muttered to himself as he drew Anne up and up towards her climax. Then, as she was *in extremis*, light cascading in aurora around her, as if she stood in the city fountain at night when the coloured changing lights were on — just at that moment, Koru drove his stunning fat penis home, deep into her body.

Anne cried out, over and over against Nadia's clit as Koru pounded into her; in, and in. His thumb pressed against her clit as she came and came: as over and over he thrust until he came. Wild and Maori warrior. Watching as Nadia came with ecstatic cries — the result of Anne's mouth sucking her. Greedily feeding from both of them Anne lay, coming and coming again, shuddering and trembling as spasms of tension came and went in her body.

Chapter 26

PHONE CALL

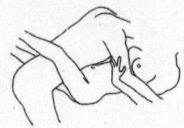

Anne lay on her bed in her new flat. The children were to come home tomorrow. She stretched and sighed contentedly. Nadia had asked her yesterday if she would consider giving up Koru and be Nadia's girlfriend exclusively.

'No,' Anne had said firmly. 'No, I can't decide between you two. How can I? It's impossible to choose! After all the stress I've had recently I don't want to have to make that kind of choice right now.' Nadia had been very understanding. Anne got the distinct impression that Nadia liked to compete with men. Little did she know that she was competing with a man who was also capable of being utterly feminine.

Last night she and Nadia had sat in on a rehearsal of Koru's version of *The Rocky Horror Picture Show*. She loved his performance. Already he had worked hard enough to be almost word-perfect. Unlike most of the other cast members he was very talented, and gorgeous and — hers. All hers.

What about Nadia? Did Anne want to have sex with her again? She giggled happily and then sighed deeply. Oh yes, more of Nadia please. She blushed when she thought of Nadia's delicious softnesses, her womanly, sexy body. The night last week when Koru had joined the two of them in bed together was a highlight of her life.

She wanted more, a lot more of both of them, preferably together if she could arrange that. How delicious it was to go from being abused by a stupid man who once declared, 'No one else on the whole planet would fancy an ugly bitch like you,' to having two lovers who competed to touch her, to kiss her, to court her with flowers and loving support. Lovers whose bodies aroused her in ways Anne had never anticipated being stimulated. Even now, just thinking about it she became turned on. She rolled over on the bed, hugging herself with joy.

The phone rang. Anne answered it, stretching in the morning sunshine as it poured through the windows.

'You bitch!' shouted Joe. 'How did you guess that I hadn't told my mates that I'd used their stories about you in my affidavit?' Anne laughed. It seemed her plan had worked.

'And . . . and . . .' he was almost speechless, choking with rage, disappointment and discovery. 'You mean to tell me that none of that stuff they told me was true? That those assholes who call themselves my friends all tried to root you and you turned them down?'

'Yep,' said Anne, feeling that further comment was unnecessary.

'It was a bit fucken mean sending your replies and their affidavits to their wives and girlfriends though,' Joe whinged. 'Most of them have rung me up and abused the fuck out of me because their girlfriend has just left them and taken *everything* because of *your* letter. Nigel came around and tried to beat me up. If I hadn't had a fridge full of beer and got him drunk I'd be in hospital by now.'

'Oh dear, how sad for you,' said Anne sympathetically, looking out at the flowers blooming in the big old-fashioned garden which lay outside her windows. 'I hope the kids didn't get to see any of this.'

'The kids are *fine* thank you. We've had a great holiday, or we would have if it hadn't been for you.'

Anne grinned, delighted with the fruit of her plan. 'Great,' she said. 'By the way, we don't need to go to court now. My lawyer has negotiated a settlement with your lawyer and from now on we will care for the kids week about.'

'How come?' Joe asked suspiciously. 'Do you trust me with them now?'

'I have to,' said Anne simply. 'You are their dad and since I've moved into Nelson we can send them to the same school. I live ten minutes away so if they need me

I'm here and if they need you the same applies.'

'But . . .' whined Joe, 'I can't get full-time work for alternate weeks and childcare costs a fortune!'

'You should have thought of that before you went for custody,' responded Anne, thinking that he sounded ever so like Sara when she was tired and ratty.

'I'm going to start studying for a degree in Information Technology. You'll have to do something like that or WINZ will kick you off the dole.'

'Shit! You smart bitch!' Joe hung up the phone by smashing it against the wall.

Anne lay on the bed trembling. She took a deep breath and blew it out slowly. I can't believe that out of 500,000 sperm, *he* was the quickest, she thought to herself as she got up off the bed and made a cup of coffee. If I'd wanted to listen to an asshole I'd have farted! Now why can't I think of things like that to say to him when he's actually on the other end of the phone?

She called Nadia up and told her about Joe's call. Nadia laughed and laughed. 'Those letters were a brilliant idea. Couldn't have given you better advice myself,' she crowed. 'I wouldn't piss in that guy's mouth if his teeth were on fire. Good on you, woman.'

Chapter 27

FRANK-N-FURTER'S FANTASIES

Koru looked long and hard at Anne as they sat in the sun outside a café. 'Wow!' he exclaimed. 'What you and I and Nadia did last week was amazing. I've always wanted to have two women in bed with me. Then there you were! Two horny women and I could at least make love with you.'

'Yeah,' said Anne. 'I think that Nadia's such a lesbian that she may not want to do the sharing thing again. She's not into men or penetration for herself. I loved it, though. Maybe I can persuade her to join us in bed again.'

'There's lots more fantasies I have that I would like to live, sometime.'

Anne looked at him and sipped her cappuccino. 'Like what? If I'm going to have a relationship with you I'd better get some idea of what your wants and needs are, what you dream about.' He nodded eagerly.

'I need to find out what I want and tell you about that too, don't I?'

'Yep. You do. I want to please you, do what you want. Pleasure you and love you and I can't read your mind so you will have to come out and tell me soon.' Koru reached out and held her hand across the café tabletop. 'God – I'm sitting here erect, wanting you. Wondering if you'll like my fantasies, dying to share them with you and yet a bit scared in case I frighten you off me.'

Anne smiled and looked deep into his eyes. 'No way, Koru. You can't put me off you. I really want to know what makes you tick and have you find that out about me too. Hell – you're the second person I've had sex with. Nadia's the third. What do *I* know about what I want and what will pleasure me? Maybe your fantasies will appeal to me and maybe not, but until you share them with me I won't know. So – what do you want to do?'

He blinked and smiled and then his eyes strayed above her head up to the tower of the cathedral which sat like a square spaceship brooding at the top end of the street.

'I've got this recurring desire to be your housemaid. I want you to order me to dress up in a silly frilly maid's outfit and make me do the washing, the ironing, scrub the floors, anything. You'd monitor my work and if it wasn't up to your standards then you'd punish me.' He sighed and squeezed her hand.

Anne laughed. 'Sounds like every solo mum's dream.

A housemaid to do the housework and give him a whack when he doesn't do it right. Gimme, gimme. Where were you *last* year?'

'I have a few bits and pieces of the outfit already. A black lace G-string, fishnet stockings, the high-heeled shoes. Now I need the dress. I want one with a full skirt and a lovely white lacy petticoat that shows off my naked bum. I'd like puffed sleeves on the dress too and a lovely frilly white apron.' Koru looked excited. His hand sweated as he held hers tightly. She didn't know whether to laugh or bite her lip. She took a deep breath.

'So I get to punish you do I? What do I get to do? Smack you on the bum or tie you up? Lock you in a room without food?'

Koru flushed. 'Well whatever you wanted to do, really. So long as it didn't actually maim me or anything like that. If I was a really good slave-girl for you then you'd reward me.'

Anne raised her eyebrows. 'Yes?'

Koru looked down and then up at her. He took a deep breath. 'I often fantasise about you sharing me with your girlfriends. Purely under your control of course. You would order me to pleasure them, or serve them food and refreshments. You would offer them my body to do with as they wished and I'd have to do it because you wanted me to.'

Anne frowned. 'I see . . .' she said, thinking furiously. 'So if you were really good at the housework I would reward you by sending you round to Tina's to do her bidding and she'd send you back when she had finished with you.' Koru nodded eagerly.

'This is different from cross-dressing, isn't it?' Anne enquired. 'It's something else, something more subtle, I suppose and what it means is I can't just be me, a helpless solo mum any more? I'd have to control *you* — control my lover?' Koru nodded vigorously, grinning all over his handsome face. 'Hmmmm, this is a new take on life for me.' Anne pushed her hair up off her face wondering how to handle this turn of events. 'So what are you offering me in return?' she asked mischievously.

'Well — what do you want, Anne? I'll do anything for you, *anything*.' Koru was the image of sincerity. She frowned and thought — and suddenly she smiled.

'I *did* have a dream about someone being my slave a month or two back. Maybe I *could* cope with you being a maid . . . *But!*' her voice became stern, 'I'd require absolute obedience, none of the stuff I put up with now — like Sara does, ignoring me. I'd want you to listen to me, pay attention, be gentle and loving. You had better be good at housework too. I'm not going to play games like this if you have really grotty standards, you know. And — and I want you to kneel at my feet.' Koru nodded eagerly. Anne was getting into her stride now.

'And I . . . I want you to give me an orgasm a day until I change my mind. I want really great sex with you. I want

223

to study what to do and how to do it and we will pleasure each other until we know utterly and completely what turns us on and what works best and how to take the longest way to our pleasure as well as the shortest way.'

Koru kissed her hand. 'Yes, mistress,' he whispered softly. 'Yes, oh yes.'

Anne looked at him. 'You *are* a kind of Frank-n-Furter, aren't you?' she realised with a small shock. He grinned, his teeth blinding in the sun.

'Yep. I think I am,' he said proudly. 'My Maori ancestors have a long history of being passionate lovers. I'm just another one of them. Do you know what my favourite line in all the show is?' Anne shook her head and drained her coffee cup of its dregs.

'It's when Frank-n-Furter seduces Brad and Janet separately in their rooms and they each think he's their lover and when they discover his disguise old Frankie says, "Yes, but isn't it *nice*?"' Koru put an utterly corrupt and lewd tone into his voice. No one could say 'nice' like that and think of England or anything but *sex*.

'Nice?' laughed Anne. 'Nice? Well none of what we do is nice by my grandmother's standards. She wouldn't like it at all.'

'Yeah,' said Koru, grinning and rubbing his hands, 'but she isn't going to get it!'

Chapter 28

HOW TO BE

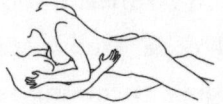

'You know, I don't know how to *be* with you. I've never been with a man who wasn't abusing me in some way.' Anne felt tears of relief and shame spring into her eyes as she admitted this thought which had been tormenting her for the past week. Twisting the tea towel around in her fingers she watched Koru put his suitcases down beside the big bed they had bought last week to put in his flat underneath Nadia's apartment.

'I – I really don't know what to do – how to treat you, I'm scared that I'll hurt you, unconsciously act towards you like I did with Joe. Had to with Joe, to survive.' She flinched as Koru stood in front of her, put his hands gently on her shoulders.

'I've got the same problem, eh?' he said, grinning widely. 'Never had a woman who could cope with me being a woman – dressing as a woman – like you do. I want to

225

come out to the whanau about it and they are sure to blame you. Can you cope with that? The ol' tangata whenua are all going to be spinning in their graves. But I don't care. You give me the strength to be who *I* am. Not who I was taught to think I *ought* to be.'

Anne smiled and relaxed her body into his, their flesh melding through their clothes as if they were soft butter poured into jeans and t-shirts, not boned bodies.

'The whanau will cope, look at Mika, he's done heaps more than you and he's becoming an honoured Maori. You're lucky, you have some idea of *who* you are. I have no idea who I am, or even who I *could* be, except a mum. I want to cook professionally but when can I begin that? I.T. is a much better bet for making money to bring up the kids.' She paused and then said teasingly, 'I could be a lesbian. Nadia wants me to be a lesbian with her.'

'Yeah, I bet she does.' Koru sounded very masculine and his eyes were laughing. 'You can be a lesbian with me, you know. We can be girlfriends together, do everything lesbian you want. You can butch-dyke or femme all you like. I won't mind. Hell I'll *love* it.' He wriggled persuasively against her in his excitement.

'Everything lesbian?' Anne asked, a sly wicked sparkle in her eyes. '*Everything*?'

Too late Koru sensed an unknown trap about to bite him on the ass but couldn't figure it out. Surrendering, he said, 'Yeah, why not. Everything.'

Anne smiled angelically and kissed Koru long and hard on his sweet warm lips. Then she went back to her kitchen across the hall and the dishes drying on the sink.

'Hey! Come on! Tell me about the everything bit!' Koru followed her and stood in front of her, arms akimbo, demanding to know with every fibre of his being what she meant.

Anne picked up a pile of side plates, carefully wiped them and slotted them home in their rack. She thought of Nadia wearing her strap-on dildo and how well she used it on Anne. How satisfying it was in her body, her mouth, everywhere. Then she saw a vision of Koru in white lingerie, lying beneath her as she parted his thighs, thrust into him, heard his oohs and ahhs of pleasure.

Everything, yes *everything* is what I want to do with you, Koru, my love. She smiled at him, knowing he'd find out soon enough. Saying nothing would inflame him more.

A loud horn beeped outside and a courier hurried up the path to the door with a parcel. Koru signed for it. 'It's for you.' He handed it to her. She felt the parcel briefly and then smiled broadly again.

'Part of the "everything" is in this parcel,' she said.

'Yeah?'

'Yes. And *you* are not allowed to open it. *I* will . . . later.' Anne firmly thrust the parcel into her pocket. It was bulky but just fitted. 'I thought you had a trailer load

227

of stuff to move sitting out there in the sun?' She raised her eyebrows at Koru.

'You're a bitch, you know that? A beeetch!' he made it sound gay. Silly and sexy all at once. He flounced out to bring in more of his things. Tip followed him, her tail wagging like a slow metronome flogging in the sun.

'Takes one to know one!' Anne called joyously to his back.

Suddenly Anne realised that she *had* changed, that she wasn't living to some programme beaten into her by Joe. She *was* in charge of her life. Astride life and riding it full tilt at a delirious gallop. She had two lovers, two lovely children and a future to look forward to.

She took the parcel from her pocket and hid it deep inside her winter coat at the back of her wardrobe. She couldn't wait to see the big fat length of the dildo she'd bought and how well it was supported by the harness she had also ordered.

Every woman in charge of her life needs a big long dildo, she thought, chuckling as she finished the dishes.

With a dildo you can fuck the world right back and never go limp.

I can't wait to see his face . . .